"*You can get what you require from any number of women.*"

"That's not only inaccurate, it's unfair. You're implying that my only interest in a woman is getting her into bed."

"Or trying to."

"I've never made a pass at you, Jessica. Doesn't that prove something?"

"That I'm not your type, obviously."

"You must be joking! I'd like to make love to you right this minute, right here on the carpet." He paused, as if in contemplation. "I'd unzip your dress and watch it slide off your shoulders, down to your hips...." His eyes held a predatory gleam as they swept over her. "You have a beautiful body."

"You haven't seen—" She stopped short, her cheeks flaming.

"Not the way I'd like to. I want to touch you, feel you come alive."

"You mustn't say such things."

"Oh, but I must. I have to correct your monumental misconception that I'm indifferent to you."

Dear Reader,

Welcome to the Silhouette **Special Edition** experience! With your search for consistently satisfying reading in mind, every month the authors and editors of Silhouette **Special Edition** aim to offer you a stimulating blend of deep emotions and high romance.

The name Silhouette **Special Edition** and the distinctive arch on the cover represent a commitment—a commitment to bring you six sensitive, substantial novels each month. In the pages of a Silhouette **Special Edition**, compelling true-to-life characters face riveting emotional issues—and come out winners. Both celebrated authors and newcomers to the series strive for depth and dimension, vividness and warmth, in writing these stories of living and loving in today's world.

The result, we hope, is romance you can believe in. Deeply emotional, richly romantic, infinitely rewarding—that's the Silhouette **Special Edition** experience. Come share it with us—six times a month!

From all the authors and editors of Silhouette **Special Edition**,

Best wishes,

Leslie Kazanjian,
Senior Editor

TRACY SINCLAIR
Willing Partners

Silhouette Special Edition

Published by Silhouette Books New York

America's Publisher of Contemporary Romance

SILHOUETTE BOOKS
300 East 42nd St., New York, N.Y. 10017

ISBN: 0-373-09584-8

First Silhouette Books printing March 1990

Printed in the U.S.A.

Books by Tracy Sinclair

TRACY SINCLAIR

Author of more than twenty-five Silhouette novels, Tracy Sinclair also contributes to various magazines and newspapers. She says her years as a photojournalist provided the most exciting adventures—and misadventures—of her life. An extensive traveler—from Alaska to South America, and most places in between—and a dedicated volunteer worker—from suicide-prevention programs to English-as-a-second-language lessons—the California resident has accumulated countless fascinating experiences, settings and acquaintances to draw on in plotting her romances.

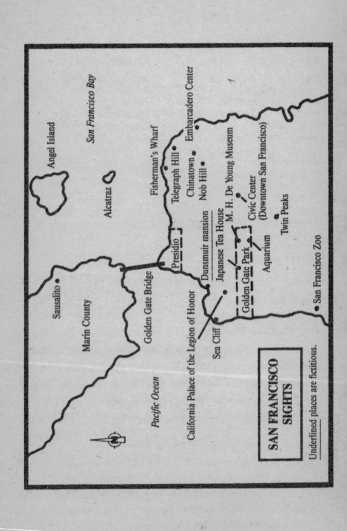

SAN FRANCISCO SIGHTS

Underlined places are fictitious.

Pacific Ocean

Marin County

Sausalito

Golden Gate Bridge

San Francisco Bay

Angel Island

Alcatraz

California Palace of the Legion of Honor

Sea Cliff

Presidio

Dunsmuir mansion

Japanese Tea House

Golden Gate Park

M. H. De Young Museum

Aquarium

Fisherman's Wharf

Telegraph Hill

Chinatown

Nob Hill

Embarcadero Center

Civic Center
(Downtown San Francisco)

Twin Peaks

San Francisco Zoo

Chapter One

Jessica Lawrence stared somberly out at the gray fog blanketing the city. It was a typical San Francisco morning.

"I'm glad it isn't sunny," she remarked to her roommate, Harriet Trent. "This is the right kind of weather for a funeral."

Harriet gazed fondly but a trifle impatiently at her friend's melancholy face. Jessica's laughing green eyes weren't sparkling now, and her generous mouth drooped. The simple dark dress she wore accurately reflected her mood, although it couldn't conceal her slender, yet curved figure.

"I'll bet you're taking the old man's death worse than his family," Harriet remarked.

"I worked for him for two years."

"Which must have set some kind of record. Before you took the job he had a different secretary every two *weeks*! Face it, Jess, Mr. Dunsmuir wasn't exactly lovable."

That wasn't a word anyone would use to describe the autocratic man she'd grown fond of, Jessica privately admitted. Winston P. Dunsmuir was used to dominating people—as much by the force of his personality as by his immense wealth. Jessica hadn't been awed by either on the day she applied for the job at his oceanfront mansion—a point in her favor, she realized later. He hated both timidity and toadying.

"You're one of the few people who could get along with the old guy," Harriet continued. "Including his own son. Will Blade Dunsmuir be at the funeral?"

"Of course. He took the first plane home."

"Where was he this time?"

"In the Near East."

"Covering another war?"

"That's what foreign correspondents do."

"It's ironic, isn't it?" Harriet asked pensively. "Blade's been over there dodging bullets for more than a year while his brother, a safe corporate lawyer, gets killed in this country."

"It was a terrible tragedy," Jessica agreed, remembering when the news came that Mr. Dunsmuir's older son and his wife had died in a car crash. That was the only time she'd seen the seemingly invincible man completely defenseless.

"You'd think it would have made him more family conscious. How he could send their poor little child away is beyond me. His only grandchild!" Harriet said indignantly.

"You make it sound like he put him in an orphanage. Kevin is in a very fine boys' school."

"The kid is only ten years old!"

"A lot of boys go away to boarding school." Jessica looked at her watch. "I'd better go or I'll be late for the funeral."

There was plenty of time, but she didn't have an adequate defense for her former employer, and loyalty prevented her from listening to criticism. She'd disapproved, too, when Mr. Dunsmuir sent Kevin away, but she understood why he'd done it. The boy was the image of his father. He had the same dark hair and gray eyes that ran in the family, plus a youthful version of the regular features that would turn rugged when he reached maturity. The older man relived his loss every time he looked at the child.

Maybe it was selfish, but he couldn't deal with the pain. Jessica was confident that he would have welcomed Kevin home in time. Unfortunately, time had run out.

After the well-attended funeral many people came back to the house to pay their condolences to the family, although Jessica suspected a preponderance of them actually came to see the house they'd heard so much about.

Winston Dunsmuir had been a very private man who shunned publicity and rarely entertained in his later years, but his stately mansion was known to contain an extensive art collection, among other treasures. Before tour buses were banned from the exclusive Sea Cliff neighborhood, his house was one of the celebrity points of interest. Tourists caught little more than a glimpse of a three-story house with mullioned glass windows, because a high brick wall enclosed the property. But that added to the legendary financier's mystique.

Sylvia Kilpatrick was looking around her brother's home with a proprietary interest. "I hope Winston left the Renoir to me," she remarked to her husband, Carter. "He knew how much I adored it."

"Blade would never miss it," he replied. "There's certainly plenty to go around." He cataloged the room with appraising eyes. "I wouldn't mind having that *bombé* chest, myself. A lot of this furniture is museum quality."

"I hope Blade appreciates it," Sylvia observed discontentedly.

"He'll undoubtedly sell the place," Carter said. "What would a bachelor like Blade want with a house this size? He doesn't spend that much time in San Francisco."

"I suppose you're right, but it seems a shame to see all these lovely things go on the auction block."

"Art objects are selling for record amounts these days. Blade should rake in millions."

"He won't need the money, and I can't help feeling that Winston would hate for his cherished possessions to go to strangers." Sylvia's thin face lit with rare animation. "Maybe he left the house to me."

"I wouldn't count on it, my dear."

"It's possible," she insisted.

Jessica listened to their exchange in silent disgust. The Kilpatricks neither needed nor deserved anything from Sylvia's brother. Their infrequent visits or phone calls were always prompted by a request of some kind, either for themselves or their two worthless children. It would surprise Jessica if they were remembered with more than a token bequest in the will. Mr. Dunsmuir had been under no illusions about his sister and her family.

Sylvia was looking at Jessica hopefully. "You were quite close to my brother. I imagine Winston discussed the terms of his will with you."

"Never," Jessica said firmly.

Carter smiled persuasively. "We both know how loyal you were to my brother-in-law, but you wouldn't be violating a confidence. It's only a matter of time until the will is read."

"Carter and I would have all kinds of decisions to make," Sylvia agreed. "For one thing, we'd have to discuss whether to move in here or sell the house. Although we'd never be able to fit all this in our apartment. Perhaps we could give the condo to the children," she mused.

"You could save Sylvia a couple of sleepless nights," Carter urged playfully.

Jessica masked her contempt with difficulty. "Whether you believe it or not, I have no knowledge of the contents of Mr. Dunsmuir's will. It would be my personal guess, however, that he left everything to his surviving son and grandchild."

Sylvia frowned. "Well, of course Winston would set up a little trust fund for Steven's child, but I doubt if he'd leave him any sizable amount. He's never been overly attached to the boy."

"Is that what you think?" Jessica smiled enigmatically and walked away. She had no more information about the will than Sylvia did, but the consternation on the older woman's face gave her great satisfaction.

Blade detached himself from a group of people as she passed by. "Can you spare a minute, Jessica?"

She paused reluctantly. Blade wasn't one of her favorite people either, although she felt sorry for him now. The deep grooves around his firm mouth and the bleakness in

his gray eyes were evidence that he was grieving for his
father. Where was he when the older man had needed
him, though? And why had their visits always been filled
with arguments?

"Everything has been so hectic that I haven't had a
chance to talk to you before. I want to thank you for all
you did for Dad," Blade said warmly. "He was very fond
of you."

"I thought a lot of him, too," Jessica answered. "I still
can't quite believe he's gone."

"I know what you mean. He always seemed indomi-
table, as though nothing could ever touch him."

"A lot of things did," she answered briefly. "He just
didn't show it."

Blade looked at her more closely. "He evidently did to
you."

"I spent a lot of time with him." Unlike the rest of
you, she added silently.

"I'd appreciate it if you'd stay on a little longer. I'm
sure my father left his affairs in perfect order, but you
know where everything is kept. Something will have to be
done with all this, too." He waved an arm at the spa-
cious living room. "Do you happen to know how he
planned to dispose of his possessions?"

Her jaw set rigidly. Was that all this family thought
about? "I have no idea, but I'm sure you'll be well taken
care of," she replied coldly.

Blade's high cheekbones became more pronounced.
His voice was glacial as he answered, "I'm quite capable
of taking care of myself without any help from my father."

Jessica fought back a withering reply, remembering the
large checks Mr. Dunsmuir had written to his son. Blade
probably thought she didn't know about those.

He looked up at the ceiling as a rhythmic, muffled sound became apparent over the voices in the crowded room. "What the devil is that?"

"I'll go and see," she offered, grateful for the interruption.

It was beneath her dignity to argue with Blade. He was a rich man's son with no sense of responsibility. When he wasn't pursuing his glamorous profession, he was romancing gorgeous women. His affairs had been well publicized by his own media. Once he came into his inheritance he could devote all his time to enjoying himself, Jessica thought waspishly.

As she reached the top of the staircase the noise became louder. It was coming from Kevin's room, the bedroom that had been his father's many years ago. Winston's grandson had been summoned from boarding school for the funeral.

Jessica's knock couldn't be heard over the din, so she opened the door. Her jaw dropped at the sight of Kevin banging away at a set of drums in accompaniment to a jazz tape.

"What do you think you're doing?" she gasped.

He looked up, unconcerned. "That's a dumb question."

She moved swiftly to turn off the cassette player. "You're old enough to know that playing the drums at a time like this is disrespectful."

His face was devoid of emotion. "What am I supposed to do?"

"Well, I...you could come downstairs and talk to your grandfather's friends."

"What for? They don't care about me anymore than he did."

Compassion replaced annoyance as she gazed at the defiant young boy. "Your grandfather loved you very much," she said gently.

"Oh, sure! That's why he sent me away to school."

"I know it's hard for you to understand right now, but it was the only thing he could do at the time."

"I understand. He didn't have room for me here." The sarcasm didn't disguise his deep hurt.

"We need to have a long talk, Kevin. Maybe I can explain some things to you."

"Why bother?" He shrugged his thin shoulders. "It's not important."

"It's extremely important. I know you don't feel like it now, but one day this week I'd like to talk to you."

"I have to go back to school tomorrow. We have a history test on Wednesday. If I miss it old man Hornsby will give me an unsatisfactory. He's just been waiting for a chance," Kevin muttered.

"You can take a make-up exam. I explained to your headmaster that you have to be here for the reading of the will."

"Why? It doesn't have anything to do with me."

"I'm sure your grandfather remembered you," Jessica said gently.

"I don't want his rotten money!" the young boy answered defiantly. "He didn't want *me*, and I don't want anything of *his*."

Her heart went out to the lonely youngster. She wished she could ease his pain, but he was in no mood to make allowances for a grandfather who seemed to have abandoned him. In Kevin's eyes his entire family had rejected him, and he wasn't far wrong.

Sylvia could have taken him in, but she'd never considered it. An heir to the Dunsmuir fortune might have been a different matter, but she couldn't foresee her brother's untimely death.

Kevin's uncle had to be faulted, too. Blade's life-style made it impossible for him to raise the boy, Jessica conceded, but he could have shown some concern. Why wasn't he up here now, reassuring Kevin? She was thoroughly disgusted with the whole clan. It shouldn't take more than a week to get everything in shape for the attorneys, and then they'd be history.

Kevin had thrown himself on the bed and was pointedly reading a comic book, so Jessica quietly left him alone. She bypassed the living room and went to the kitchen to speak to Mrs. Bartlett, the housekeeper.

"Could you send a tray up to Kevin's room?" she asked the pleasant-faced older woman. "I don't think he feels like coming down to dinner."

"I'm not surprised, poor little lamb. First he loses his parents, and now his grandfather."

"I wouldn't try to talk to him about it right now," Jessica said carefully. "He's taking it rather badly."

"And who can blame him? But don't you worry, I'll take good care of that boy."

Jessica got her raincoat from the closet, intending to leave unobtrusively. On her way to the front door she was stopped by Grant Sutherland, the family attorney. He was tall and distinguished, with graying temples, the stereotypical senior partner of a conservative law firm—except for the slightly irreverent gleam in his eyes. He and Winston Dunsmuir had enjoyed a friendship as well as a business relationship for decades.

"It was a nice turnout today," he remarked. "Winston would have been pleased."

"Do you really think so?"

Sutherland laughed. "No, he wouldn't have given a damn, but it seemed like the right thing to say."

"I'm going to miss him," Jessica said poignantly.

"I am, too."

After a moment of shared silence she said, "I'll stay on as long as you need me, of course, but I hope it won't take long to wind up his affairs."

The older man looked at her speculatively. "Do you have another job lined up?"

"No, I haven't even thought about it yet. I'll probably take a week or two off before I start looking."

"That sounds sensible."

"Well, I'm going to leave now." She held out her hand. "I know we'll talk on the phone, but if I don't see you again, I've enjoyed our association."

"You can't get rid of a lawyer that easily," he joked. "I'll see you at the reading of the will on Thursday."

"I don't have any reason to be there."

"Weren't you notified? I can't be specific, naturally, but you're mentioned in the will."

She stared at him in surprise. "Why would Mr. Dunsmuir leave me anything? I was only in his employ for two years."

"We're jumping the gun a little. I'm not free to tell you anything except that your name is mentioned." As someone came over to speak to him, the attorney said, "Plan to be in my office at ten on Thursday morning."

Jessica couldn't help speculating on her possible inheritance as she drove home. It was totally unexpected. Her relationship with the wealthy financier had always been businesslike, although he did discuss his family with her occasionally. He'd also asked about her own goals and ambitions, but casually, the way anybody would show an interest in someone they saw every day. Whatever he left her had to be trivial, just a keepsake.

When Jessica arrived for work the next morning, Blade was having breakfast alone in the dining room. He was dressed in tight jeans and a chest-hugging T-shirt, both of which displayed his excellent physique. Not an ounce of fat padded his lean body.

"Will you join me for breakfast?" he asked.

"No thanks, I never eat breakfast."

"Is that how you stay in shape?" His eyes went over her slender figure admiringly.

Jessica was annoyed by his blatant masculine appraisal. She knew about Blade's reputation as a charmer, but all that macho sex appeal didn't impress her one bit.

"I'll be in the den if you need me," she said coolly.

"Have a cup of coffee at least," he coaxed. "I hate to eat alone."

"Where's Kevin?"

"I don't know. I haven't seen him this morning."

Or last night, either, she commented silently. "Perhaps I should see if he's all right. He's a very troubled young boy."

"I don't doubt it, poor kid."

"You're his uncle, one of his few remaining relatives. Don't you think it would be nice if you spent some time with him?"

Blade frowned. "I've tried to talk to him, but it's like talking to a door. He refuses to communicate. I've never met a child like that."

"How many children have you met?" she asked scornfully.

Something flickered in his eyes. "More than I've wanted to at times."

"Then why are you surprised at Kevin's lack of warmth? Children can tell when you don't like them."

"That's not what I said." He stared at her without expression. "You don't like me, Miss Lawrence. May I ask why?"

"I'm just an employee here, Mr. Dunsmuir. My opinion of you doesn't matter one way or the other."

"That's correct," he answered arrogantly. "I'm merely curious. To the best of my knowledge, you don't know anything about me."

"You're too modest. Your activities have been splashed all over the newspapers."

He looked amused. "Since you can scarcely object to my work, I presume it's my personal life that bothers you."

"Nothing about you bothers me," she stated firmly. "If you want to spend your free time partying all night, that's your business. I don't happen to find playboys particularly palatable."

"I've never considered myself a playboy. I work for a living the same as you do."

"I'd scarcely call our jobs comparable. Mine rarely brings me in contact with the jet set."

His eyes narrowed dangerously. "Have you ever covered a war, Miss Lawrence? Do you *really* know the terrible cost in lives and devastation? Have you ever seen women and children maimed?"

She was shaken by his sudden intensity. The amused dilettante had turned into a coldly implacable inquisitor. "I . . . I suppose it must be horrible," she faltered.

"That doesn't begin to describe it. You want to run away and pretend it's not happening, but you can't. So you do the next best thing. You have a few drinks and inhale the perfume of a beautiful woman instead of the stench of war. And sometimes you can forget for a few hours.''

"I'm sorry, Mr. Dunsmuir," she said in a muted voice. "I had no right to say what I did."

His jaw remained rigid for a moment. It relaxed when he smiled. "Don't you think we'd be better friends if we were back on a first-name basis?"

"Whatever you say," she agreed, anxious to atone.

"That's a dangerous offer, considering my appetite for gorgeous women," he said mischievously.

His sudden switch to suggestiveness made her realize how tricky he was. Jessica was furious at herself for considering Blade a romantic figure, however briefly. No doubt all that talk about the horrors of war was a glib story he fed to gullible women. It was more likely that he filed his copy from a comfortable bar, far from the combat zone.

"I'm not gorgeous, and you're not interested in me," she said stiffly. "If you want to stay in practice, go find someone who has time to play games with you."

"A lot of my father rubbed off on you." He chuckled.

"I admired him very much."

"So did I, but I could see his faults. That's why we fought so much."

"You were entirely blameless, I suppose?" she asked ironically.

"Not at all. I inherited his short fuse, but at least I don't try to tell other people how to live their lives."

"I guess parents can't help doing that."

"But Dad wasn't the kind to give up," Blade answered moodily. "He wanted me to come home and settle down. That's what most of our arguments were about."

"He was very lonely," Jessica said softly. "Especially after your brother died."

"I couldn't take Steven's place. We were two different people."

"You have to assume responsibility now. You're the only one left."

"Don't worry, I'll see that Kevin is well taken care of."

"He needs more than material things," Jessica said urgently. "He doesn't think anybody cares about him. Kevin is really feeling sorry for himself."

Blade's face darkened. "He's better off than a lot of kids I know."

"How can you be so callous?" she gasped.

"You get that way after a while if you want to survive."

"I would think you'd have more feeling for your brother's son."

"I do, damn it! I just don't know what to do for him."

"Well, maybe if—" She broke off abruptly as Kevin came into the dining room. "Good morning. Are you ready for breakfast?" she asked brightly.

"That's what I'm here for." His answer stopped just short of being insolent.

Blade's teeth clicked together, but he made an effort to be pleasant. "Try the French toast. It's great."

"I don't like French toast," Kevin answered.

"What would you rather have?" Jessica asked. "Mrs. Bartlett will make anything you want."

"A peanut-butter-and-jelly sandwich."

"For breakfast?"

He unfolded his napkin with elaborate patience. "I knew I wouldn't get it."

"If that's what you really want, of course you can have it," Jessica said.

"After breakfast, how would you like to go to the zoo?" Blade asked.

"No thank you," Kevin answered.

"They have a new monkey house that's supposed to be fantastic," Jessica remarked.

When he didn't answer, Blade said, "How about going to Chinatown, then? I still remember a wooden abacus I got there when I was about your age. Have you ever seen a shopkeeper add a column of figures on one of those gadgets?"

"No."

"That sounds like fun," Jessica said quickly, aware of Blade's dwindling patience. "I wish I could come with you."

"You're welcome to come along," Blade said. "How about it, Kevin?"

"No thank you," the boy repeated.

"What *would* you like to do?" Jessica asked.

"I guess I'll just hang out on the beach."

"That's an even better idea," Blade said. "I'll go with you. We can bat a volleyball around."

"You don't have to baby-sit me," Kevin answered scornfully.

"That wasn't my intention. I'm only going to be here for a week, and I'd like to get to know you better. You're my only nephew."

"Big deal," Kevin muttered.

"It *is* a big deal. Your father and I were good buddies, besides being brothers. I know how much you miss him, because I miss him, too."

"You never even think about him. None of you do!" Kevin fought back tears as he stood up abruptly. "All of you wish I'd go away, too." He rushed out of the room.

"Now you know what I'm up against," Blade said bleakly. "He's been that way since I got here."

"You can't give up," Jessica pleaded. "He's so desperately unhappy."

He sighed. "I don't think I can do much about it in a week."

Blade's misgivings were well-founded. Kevin was like a mournful ghost in the house. He kept to himself and spoke only when spoken to, and then as briefly as possible. Most of the time he wandered aimlessly around on the beach below the house, kicking at the sand. Jessica watched helplessly from the den window.

With the twin distractions of Kevin and Blade, she didn't get much work done. Both of them disturbed her in different ways. She looked forward to the reading of the will. That was all that was keeping them there. After they left she could get on with her own life.

As she was preparing to leave her apartment on Thursday morning the telephone rang.

"I ran into a bit of a problem here," Blade informed her. "Kevin refuses to go to the attorney's office with me."

"I guess the whole thing sounds intimidating. Just explain that it's only a formality."

"I did, but he won't budge. He says he's sick."

"Is he?"

"Not as far as I can see."

"What's he complaining of?"

"You name it," Blade answered succinctly. "Headache, upset stomach, the works."

Jessica's brow furrowed. "That sounds like the flu. Is he warm? Do you think he has a temperature?"

"His bottom would be warm if I had *my* way," Blade muttered. "There's nothing wrong with him. He's well enough to watch television, and savvy enough to hide the bag of potato chips he was eating when he heard me coming."

"Then simply tell him you know he's faking, and it won't do him any good because he has to go with you."

"Is that the best you can do?" Blade asked disgustedly. "The only way I'm going to get that kid to Sutherland's office is to sling him over my shoulder and carry him in."

"You can't do that!"

"Do you have a better suggestion?"

"Well, I ... uh ..."

"I thought so," he said dryly.

"I don't imagine it's essential for him to be there. If he's that upset about it, let him stay home."

"This ten-year-old you're so worried about is outwitting both of us." Blade slammed down the phone.

All of the family were assembled in the lawyer's office when Jessica arrived. The Dunsmuir household staff was also there, and a few people she didn't recognize. The will evidently contained many bequests.

Underneath the obligatory solemn atmosphere was a feeling of anticipation. Sylvia made a stab at masking her eagerness, but her two children didn't bother to make any pretense.

Jessica had only a nodding acquaintance with them, but she knew Mr. Dunsmuir hadn't approved of either one. Larry Kilpatrick was a year older than Blade, which would make him about thirty-six. He was conventionally handsome, with a surface charm that concealed an enormous ego. His goal in life was to become rich without working at it, although he held a job with a well-known real estate firm. They tolerated his halfhearted efforts because Larry occasionally sold a high-priced property to one of his socially prominent friends.

Nina Kilpatrick wasn't any more of a bargain than her brother. She was a chic, brittle woman with a patronizing manner toward people she considered socially inferior, like Jessica. For lack of anything better to do, Nina drifted from one uninspired job to another. All were secured through her parents' influence, and none were to her liking. At present she was a fashion consultant at a pricy specialty shop. Like her brother, she depended mostly on her friends for sales.

Larry strolled over to Jessica as she paused near the door. "I didn't expect to see you here," he commented.

"Mr. Sutherland asked me to come."

"That's interesting." His eyes lit with a calculating gleam. "Maybe you'll walk out of here an heiress."

"Don't worry, I seriously doubt it."

"There's plenty to go around. The old boy was loaded."

She glanced over the room instead of responding to his tasteless remark. "Isn't Blade here yet?"

Larry's smile was unpleasant. "I gather you think he's a better prospect."

"For what?" she asked, her temper beginning to rise.

"You two must have gotten pretty chummy this week, all alone in the house together."

"All alone with the staff and Kevin."

"You're a clever girl. Where there's a will there's a way." He chuckled at his own wit. "But when Blade comes into his inheritance he's going to have women swarming all over him. You'd be better off setting your sights lower." His gaze traveled over her slim body, lingering on her firm breasts. "I always figured you wouldn't give me a break because you were afraid Uncle Winston would disapprove, but that's no problem anymore."

Before Jessica could tell him the approximate date in the next century when she'd be willing to "give him a break," his mother bustled over.

"Where is Blade?" Sylvia asked querulously. "Surely he couldn't have gotten the time wrong?"

"No, he'll be here. I spoke to him before I left," Jessica said. "He's having trouble with Kevin."

"I'd forgotten about the boy. What's wrong?"

"He didn't want to come."

"That's sensible. This is no place for a child."

"He's probably one of the heirs, Mother," Larry pointed out.

"Not one of the major ones, surely," Sylvia said dismissively. "Whatever small amount he's left will be held in trust anyway."

Nina joined them. "What's going on?"

"We were discussing your little cousin Kevin," her mother said.

"Where is he? And where's Blade? I'd like to get this show on the road so I can find out if I'm rich enough to quit my job."

"Unless Winston was exceptionally generous, you're not to do anything hasty, Nina," Sylvia implored. "Your father and I went to a lot of trouble to get you that position."

"Too bad you couldn't get her a rich husband instead," Larry drawled.

"I don't notice *you* marrying an heiress," Nina answered furiously.

"I have a better chance, sister dear."

"If you can find someone feeble-minded."

"Children, stop this immediately!" Sylvia ordered. "Remember where you are."

Blade's arrival provided a welcome diversion, although his mood wasn't encouraging. This was not a happy occasion, and losing an argument to a ten-year-old hadn't improved matters. Nina would have done well not to challenge him, but sensitivity wasn't one of her virtues.

"Where have you been?" she demanded. "Everyone's anxious to get on with the reading of the will."

"Everyone?" he asked cynically. "Or you and Larry?"

"We were getting worried about you, dear," Sylvia said.

"That's right, Cousin. We wouldn't want anything to happen to you," Larry said mockingly.

Jessica had suspected that Blade didn't have a very high regard for his cousins, an opinion he shared with his late father. She now discovered there was no love lost on either side.

"Is Kevin all right?" she asked, to avert a further clash between Blade and Larry.

"That depends on your viewpoint," Blade answered curtly. "I wouldn't be surprised if he burned the house down while we're gone."

"You left him home all alone?"

"What else could I do? Mrs. Bartlett and Hawkins were told to be here. Where was I supposed to get a sitter at the last minute? Assuming I even knew of one."

Hawkins was the butler, a devoted man who had been in the Dunsmuir employ for many years. Naturally he'd be remembered in the will and asked to be there along with the housekeeper, but Jessica hoped Kevin didn't feel abandoned.

"The child will be fine," Sylvia said. "He isn't a baby. Besides, he won't be alone long."

"He's already been alone *too* long," Jessica said before walking away.

They all looked up expectantly as Grant Sutherland entered the room. "If everyone is here, I believe we can get started," he announced.

"Kevin isn't here," Jessica told him. "Blade intended to bring him, but he said he didn't feel well."

"A rather sudden illness?"

"Not really." She lowered her voice. "Let's face it, he hasn't had much reason to want to be with his family."

"Winston loved the boy," Sutherland said gently.

"I know." Jessica sighed. "The problem is convincing Kevin of that."

"Perhaps he'll realize it soon."

"I hope Kevin is well taken care of, but that won't change his mind. Leaving him money will be a meaningless gesture as far as he's concerned. What he really wanted—still wants—is affection."

"Some people find that difficult to give. They keep it all bottled up inside like my dear friend Winston. I hope some day Kevin will come to understand his grandfather."

"I hope so, too," Jessica answered without conviction. "It's not essential that he be here today, is it? I mean, you won't have to postpone the reading? I'd like this to be my last contact with the Dunsmuir family."

The attorney's expression was enigmatic. "We can proceed without the boy. As a matter of fact, it might be better this way."

Larry joined them. "What's holding up the performance? I want to get my loot to the bank before it closes."

"Your levity is out of place, Lawrence," his mother admonished. "He always uses humor to cover his true feelings," she remarked to the older man.

"A sense of humor is a valuable thing to have. I hope he never loses it." A mischievous smile lit Sutherland's face for a moment before being replaced by his customary dignity. Raising his voice slightly to get attention, he said, "Ladies and gentlemen, if you'll all take a seat, we can proceed with the reading of Winston Dunsmuir's will."

Chapter Two

The atmosphere in the paneled law office was one of happy expectancy as everyone looked at the distinguished man behind the polished desk. His voice was uninflected as he began to speak.

"You were asked to come here today because you are all mentioned in Winston Dunsmuir's last will and testament. Before we begin, I must advise you that any person contesting the provisions set forth will automatically forfeit his or her claim to the estate. Is that quite clear?"

Everyone except the close relatives bobbed their heads automatically. The Kilpatricks looked at each other with dawning concern, while Blade stared out at the gray drizzle with a scowl on his face.

"If that's understood, we can begin." The attorney put on a pair of black-rimmed glasses and picked up the legal document.

The first part of the will dealt with sizable bequests to numerous charities. Jessica knew how generous her employer had been, but it came as a small shock to his family. Sylvia and her brood looked disapproving yet not actually alarmed, since they knew what a vast sum remained.

Larry couldn't resist a sotto voce comment, however. "Didn't he ever hear that charity begins at home?"

"You don't get public credit for it," Nina answered cynically.

When Sutherland glanced up, Sylvia whispered, "Hush, children. Be patient."

After the charitable donations came bequests to the many people who had worked for Winston Dunsmuir. They were handsomely rewarded according to their years of service. Many could now afford to retire, including Hawkins and Mrs. Bartlett.

Jessica kept waiting to hear her name, although she didn't expect anything on a scale with the others. When the long list came to an end, however, she hadn't been mentioned.

"The next bequest is to Kevin Dunsmuir," Sutherland read. "To my beloved grandson, Kevin Dunsmuir, I leave half of my estate, which includes all money and property, to be held in trust for him until he reaches the age of twenty-one. I appoint my son, Blade Dunsmuir, to act as guardian during this period. All living expenses for my grandson will be paid for out of the trust fund, which will be administered by Grant Sutherland. It is my further wish that Kevin shall reside in the house at 418 Ocean View Drive."

During the measured reading Sylvia and her husband exchanged stunned glances. The large bequest was a nasty surprise.

"I can't believe Winston would leave half his estate to a child he regarded as a mere obligation," she murmured. "He didn't even want the boy around."

"'Conscience does make cowards of us all,'" Larry answered mockingly in a rare literate moment. "Maybe the old sinner figured he was buying his way into heaven."

Sylvia was too disturbed to admonish him. She was busy calculating. "That only leaves half to be divided among all of us, and Blade hasn't been mentioned yet."

"To continue," Sutherland said calmly over the small disturbance. "I leave the other half of my estate to my son, Blade, under the following conditions. He is to reside in the family home with his nephew, Kevin, for a period of one year. At the end of that time he will receive one-half of his inheritance. If he refuses to reside there for a year, he will forfeit all money and property, which will then be distributed in equal shares between my sister, Sylvia Kilpatrick, and her children, Lawrence and Nina Kilpatrick. If Blade marries within said year, he will inherit the remaining quarter of my estate. If he agrees to the year's residency clause but fails to marry within that period, the remaining one quarter will be distributed to the aforementioned heirs."

The room erupted into angry recriminations. Blade was the most furious. "That manipulative, conniving old—" The words were bitten off with an effort.

"This is not to be believed! How could my own brother be so treacherous?" Sylvia moaned. "How could he cut off his nearest and dearest without a cent?"

"He was obviously not in his right mind," Carter declared, angry color mottling his cheekbones.

"I assure you, he was," Sutherland answered calmly.

"The old goat is probably laughing is head off," Nina said sullenly.

"Well, I don't know about the rest of you, but I'm not going to take this lying down." Larry's face was ugly. "I'm going to fight for my rights."

"What can we do?" Nina asked. "The will says we can't benefit if we sue."

"So what? He didn't leave us anything anyway."

"He did if Blade doesn't fulfill the terms of the will." Sister and brother stared at their cousin in a new light.

Grant Sutherland tried to quell the uprising. "Please bear with me a little longer, ladies and gentlemen. I'm not quite finished. There is one more paragraph in the will. It concerns Jessica Lawrence."

Jessica was so bemused by the strange turn of events that she'd forgotten the fact that she hadn't been mentioned yet. The terms of the will were patently unfair to Blade. How could Mr. Dunsmuir restrict his son's inheritance in that manner? It didn't make sense. He was punishing a son he adored, while rewarding relatives who didn't deserve consideration. If she hadn't known better, Jessica would have agreed with Carter's appraisal. But Winston Dunsmuir hadn't been senile. What on earth was on his mind when he made out that will?

The enforced silence in the room pulsated with resentment as the attorney read the final provision. "I request my secretary, Jessica Lawrence, to remain in my employ for one year after my death, the amount of time I estimate it will take to catalog my library, which is to be given to Stanford University. She will live in the house on Ocean View Drive until the job is completed. During this period of time she is to be paid the sum of one thousand dollars per week. If she refuses this offer, someone else shall be hired to undertake the task."

Jessica stared at the attorney numbly. It didn't take much calculation to figure out she was being offered more than fifty thousand dollars for a year's work. Winston could have gotten someone to do the job for a fraction of that amount. Did he realize she'd feel uncomfortable with such a large gift? Gossip could be cruel, even where there was no basis for it. Under the terms he proposed, she would be performing a valid service, albeit an overpaid one. Was this his way of rewarding her loyalty without having anyone question their relationship?

"That concludes the reading of the will, ladies and gentlemen," Sutherland said while she was puzzling over her part in it.

Everyone filed out of the office except the immediate family and Jessica. She remained in her chair while the rest of them attacked the attorney with angry accusations.

"I won't do it!" Blade declared. "He's still trying to rule my life, but I won't permit it."

"That's your privilege," Sutherland answered imperturbably.

"Some privilege! Dad knew what that money meant to me."

"It's yours if you fulfill the conditions he set down."

"Give up my job? That's a hell of a choice."

"Only for a year," Sutherland said. "You can pursue your career in this country for that length of time."

"Why should I? Because my father wanted me out of the combat area so I wouldn't get hurt? What difference does it make now that he's gone?"

"A lot to your nephew. Winston wanted him to have a home."

"So I'm supposed to marry a nice girl, go to work from nine to five, and the three of us will live happily ever after?"

"That's up to you," the older man said without emotion.

"Oh, is it?" Blade asked sarcastically. "The millions of dollars involved if I don't roll over like a good dog aren't meant to influence me?"

"I don't think it's unreasonable to expect you to perform a small service for the considerable rewards involved."

"You consider a year of my life a small service?"

"If you find it too much of a hardship, you can forfeit your inheritance," Sutherland answered impassively.

"Winston has been terribly unfair." Sylvia had been waiting to get a word in. "I wouldn't blame you one bit if you contested the will," she told Blade.

"I wouldn't advise it," Sutherland said.

"Any court in the land would rule that Winston was of unsound mind when he wrote that thing." Carter repeated his earlier assertion.

"Can I take it that you intend to institute a lawsuit?" Sutherland asked.

Carter's eyes swiveled away from the other man's direct gaze. "It's Blade I'm concerned about. My family aren't really beneficiaries."

"Oh, what the hell! It was his money. He can do whatever he wants with it." Blade stormed out of the room.

"I wonder what that means?" Larry asked, staring after him.

"Don't get your hopes up, brother dear," Nina answered. "Blade's not going to blow millions. When he calms down he'll be a good little boy and stick it out for a year."

"I'm not so sure," Sylvia remarked thoughtfully. "Blade has made quite a name for himself in his field, and a year can be a long time."

"Not when you spend it looking for a wife," Nina observed. "Take my word for it, he'll be married in a matter of months."

"I have to agree with Nina, even though it may be the first time," Larry said. "Our best bet is to start hunting up a good lawyer. What do we have to lose?"

Carter gave Sutherland an uneasy look. "That kind of talk is premature. Your mother and I will have to discuss this."

"I'm still in shock," Sylvia agreed. "To think that my brother could play such a shabby trick. It would serve Winston right if I did question the validity of the will, much as I would hate to air our dirty linen in court."

"For that kind of cash we can afford to get a little dirty," Larry said.

"It would be quite distasteful, besides being unfair to Blade." Sylvia gazed innocently at Sutherland, who had taken little part in the conversation. "Litigation can drag on so long, and that would tie up Blade's inheritance, wouldn't it?"

"Since I'm the executor of the will, I'm not at liberty to give any answers that might jeopardize my client's interests," he responded smoothly. "I suggest you put any questions to your own attorney."

"Oh, I haven't—I mean, I don't want to do anything hasty."

Jessica was beginning to understand Sylvia's strategy. A lawsuit would be costly, with no guarantee of success. It would tie up the estate, however. Blade might be willing to make a settlement in order to avoid such a possibility.

"If you'll excuse me, I'd like to have a word with Miss Lawrence," Sutherland said. As the Kilpatricks filed out of the room arguing animatedly among themselves, he came over to Jessica. "I'm glad you waited," he told her.

"I guess I was too stunned to leave."

He smiled sardonically. "Winston's will does seem to have provoked strong emotions."

"I admired him very much, but I have to say that a lot of the conditions seem unfair."

"A person is entitled to leave his money any way he chooses."

"But not to use it as a reward or punishment. He loved Blade. How could he turn his life upside down?"

"He loved Kevin, too. Perhaps Winston felt they both needed a home."

"I don't know how that arrangement will work out," she said dubiously. "They don't get along very well."

"Because they barely know each other, which is a pity. The Dunsmuir family has dwindled down to a precious few."

"Is that the reason for the marriage clause?"

Sutherland's face didn't give anything away. "All parents want their children to marry and settle down," he answered blandly.

"But they don't usually *force* them to do it. Frankly, I'm very disappointed in Mr. Dunsmuir. Blade should be allowed to take his time and choose the wife he really wants."

The attorney seemed amused. "I've known him a lot longer than you have, Jessica, and I can assure you that's exactly what he'll do."

"That much money could be a powerful incentive."

"Not necessarily. A quarter of the estate would more than satisfy his needs."

"You think he'll put his job on hold for a year?"

"I'm almost certain of it. I know how much he wants that money."

Jessica knew it was wrong to judge Blade. Most people would change their life-style for a lot less, and he wasn't exactly being asked to rough it. The whole concept was slightly repugnant, however. Blade hadn't seemed like the kind of man who could be dictated to.

"How about you?" Sutherland asked. "Are you going to accept the job?"

"I don't see how I can turn it down."

"Excellent. That's what Winston hoped you would say."

"He must have been darn sure of it when he offered that kind of salary. Why did he, when he could have gotten someone for so much less?" she asked, curious.

"Cataloging his extensive library is very meticulous work," Sutherland answered smoothly. "Winston wanted the job done right, and he had great confidence in your ability."

Jessica didn't think that was the full explanation, but she refrained from pursuing the matter. "Well, I'm very grateful. For the first time in my life I'll be able to save a sizable amount of money."

"Especially since all your living expenses will be paid," he agreed.

"Oh, I'm not going to move into the house. I'll pass on that part of it."

"I don't think you quite understand. That was one of the conditions of the job."

"I didn't interpret it that way. What difference does it make where I live? I'll go in every morning the way I always have."

"I'm sorry, but that won't be possible."

"I'm sure Mr. Dunsmuir was simply offering me the option," she insisted. "You're just being arbitrary."

"Believe me, Jessica, I have no leeway in the matter. Winston made his wishes clear."

"You talked about this together?" she demanded.

"I have to administer the terms of the will exactly as they were written," he answered noncommittally.

"This puts a new face on things," she muttered.

He watched her with the lack of expression seen on high-stakes poker players. "You have the same free choice as Blade."

"And the same problem. This would change my life, too."

"Would you like a little time to think it over?"

Her first impulse was to say yes, but postponing the decision wouldn't make it any easier. The conditions of employment were unreasonable, yet moving into the Dunsmuir mansion wouldn't be a hardship. Except that Blade would be there, too. They weren't what you could call soul mates now, and living together could heighten the friction that already flared between them on occasion. They wouldn't really be *living* together, though, and in a house that large they could surely avoid each other. Days might go by without their ever meeting. It was just the suddenness of the idea that made her so uneasy.

"You don't have to make up your mind this minute," Sutherland said.

"I might as well." She drew a deep breath. "I'll take the job—conditions and all."

"Splendid! Winston would be pleased. He was very fond of you."

He had a strange way of showing affection, Jessica thought resentfully. Was her former employer really a generous man, or was he playing some elaborate joke from beyond the grave? She had the uncomfortable feeling that she was about to walk into a trap—velvet-lined, but a trap nonetheless.

"Maybe you'd better tell Blade first," she said hesitantly. "He's had enough shocks for one day."

"I'm sure he'll consider this the turning point in his fortunes," the older man said gallantly.

Jessica had rather assumed that Hawkins and Mrs. Bartlett would retire on their pensions. She was relieved to learn that neither had any intention of leaving.

"I wouldn't walk out when I'm needed," Mrs. Bartlett declared. "We're going to have a full house around here."

"If you need more help, I'm sure it won't be a problem," Jessica said. "I'll speak to Mr. Sutherland."

"I wasn't complaining. It will be nice to have young people around again like in the old days. Mr. Blade and his brother weren't much older than Kevin when I first came to work here." The housekeeper's eyes were tender with reminiscence. "What a pair of scamps they were. Always getting into some kind of mischief and charming their way out of it."

"It's a pity Kevin doesn't take after either of them," Jessica observed soberly.

"The boy has their ways," Mrs. Bartlett assured her. "He's going through a bad patch right now, but he'll come out of it."

Jessica didn't share her confidence. In the few days she'd been there, Kevin had continued to be remote. The only emotion he'd shown was after being told he wasn't returning to boarding school. Then he'd thrown a minor tantrum.

If these first days were indicative of the months ahead, she'd made a bad decision, Jessica reflected. Blade was as difficult to live with as Kevin. He hung around the house all day wearing a perpetual scowl.

Jessica found it hard to work under those conditions, although she couldn't complain about distractions. The house was very quiet—unnaturally so. It was the brooding kind of silence that presaged a storm. Her attention kept wandering, and Jessica wondered what would set off the explosion.

When Kevin started school on Monday the strain should be relieved somewhat. But what were Blade's plans? If he had any, he wasn't sharing them with her. Not that they had much contact. About the only time she saw him was at meals, and that had been her idea. Jessica had discussed living arrangements with Blade when she'd first moved in.

"This situation isn't what any of us would have chosen, but since we're stuck with each other, I propose we make things as easy as possible," she began.

"Oh, God, I'm living with Mary Poppins," he muttered.

"Hardly," Jessica answered crisply. "I have no interest in playing nursemaid to you. I was referring to Mrs. Bartlett. She isn't being paid to run a hotel for our convenience. I was suggesting we have our meals together so she can maintain some kind of schedule, instead of having to serve each of us separately."

"That makes sense," Blade admitted.

"It would also give Kevin a sense of normality if we ate together as a family."

"One like the Munsters?" he asked derisively. "That's the only family the kid would fit into."

Jessica had defended Kevin, but she had to admit privately that Blade was right. The boy resisted every effort to make life more bearable. He never entered into a conversation, and he answered questions in monosyllables. She finally got a response out of him at dinner on Sunday night, but not a positive one.

They were having dessert when she remarked brightly, "We'd better leave here about eight-thirty tomorrow morning. The school is only ten minutes away, but getting you enrolled will take a little time."

"You don't have to go with me. I can go by myself." Kevin's reply was lengthier than any of his responses all evening.

"Would you prefer to have me take you?" Blade asked.

"I don't need either of you."

"I'm sure you could manage adequately on your own, but you can't simply drop in and say, here I am. The school system requires an adult to fill out a lot of forms." Blade tried to keep his voice pleasant.

"You're just afraid I won't go if you don't keep an eye on me."

"We realize it's difficult to make a change in the middle of the term, but you have to go to school," Jessica said gently.

"Sure, just like I have to do everything else a bunch of strangers decide," Kevin answered bitterly. "Nobody cares what *I* want." He shoved back his chair and left the room before they could stop him.

"We all know what he wants, but how can you give him back his parents?" Blade asked somberly. "I only wish I could convince him that things will get better."

"You aren't setting a very good example," Jessica said quietly.

"What do you want me to do?"

"Almost anything would be helpful. You've been moping around the house just like Kevin, but with less reason. You grew up here. You have a lot of friends who want to help."

The phone had rung steadily since Blade had been home, but he hadn't shown any inclination to resume old acquaintanceships. Not even with the women with sexy voices. Jessica usually answered the telephone, so she knew that half the callers were female.

"I'm not in any mood to socialize," he answered curtly.

"I wasn't suggesting a wild evening of drinking and carousing, but a quiet dinner with friends would do you good. Your father wouldn't want you to cut yourself off completely this way."

He smiled sardonically. "You mean he'd want me to get on with my life?"

"Yes, certainly."

"Then perhaps you can explain why he preempted a year of it?" Blade's dark humor was replaced by frustration. "In spite of all our differences of opinion, we loved and respected each other. I'm going to miss him like the very devil, yet I find it difficult to forgive him for what he's done to me. The thing I don't understand is why he did it!"

"I'm sure it was out of concern for your safety," she soothed.

"That doesn't make sense. All he managed to do was sidetrack me for a while. He must have known I'd have my bags packed on the day the year was up."

"You might change your mind. A lot can happen in a year," Jessica said vaguely. She didn't know any better than Blade what had gone through his father's mind.

"That obviously accounts for the second carrot in front of my nose. If his plans work out, I'll meet a nice girl, settle down here and raise Kevin. Then all the loose ends will be neatly tied in a bow."

"Would that be so terrible?"

"You're damn right it would! I'll marry when I please, not to satisfy a meddlesome old man who always had to have the last word."

"Whether it was fair or not, this wasn't a frivolous decision on your father's part," Jessica protested.

"No, I'm sure he put a lot of thought into it, but he overlooked one thing. What's to prevent me from marrying simply to fulfill the terms of the will?" He looked at her speculatively. "It shouldn't be difficult to find a woman interested in a straight business proposition."

Jessica's green eyes narrowed. "If you're thinking about me, forget it!"

A little smile curved his firm mouth. "You haven't heard my offer yet."

"And I don't care to," she snapped.

"Don't be hasty, Jessica," he said softly. "We're two of a kind. Dad bought you the same way he bought me."

"That's not true! It isn't the same at all," she sputtered. "I simply agreed to continue working here."

"Under rather unusual conditions. I'm flattered that you didn't feel living with me would be a hardship," he said mockingly.

Jessica realized a lot of women would have taken the job for that privilege alone. Blade was potently masculine as he lounged in the chair, his athlete's body deceptively relaxed. He was a magnificent specimen of manhood in the prime of life.

"I'll admit I'm not thrilled about the living arrangements," she explained carefully. "But it's a small price... I mean, Mr. Dunsmuir would have wanted me to..."

Blade raised a peaked eyebrow at her halting justification. "At least I'm honest about my motives."

"All right, I'm here because I want the money," she flared. "But I'm going to earn it."

"You think I'm not?" His gaze went over her appraisingly. "I wonder if you were Dad's choice to domesticate me."

"Definitely not. He once told me I was the most independent woman he'd ever known."

"Sounds like a compliment to me."

"He was annoyed when he said it," Jessica answered succinctly.

Blade chuckled. "I told you he hated to lose an argument."

"In that case, I certainly wouldn't be his choice. You'll have to look elsewhere for a business partner."

His laughter faded. "Dad didn't make an error in judgment. He knew I would never pull a trick like that."

Jessica's spirits rose for no discernible reason. Blade meant nothing to her. Their paths had crossed through the caprice of an old man. When the year was up they might not even be on speaking terms. Still, she was glad he was showing integrity.

Her voice was gentler as she said, "Have you thought about what you're going to do for a year?"

"What does a war correspondent do on sabbatical?" he countered wryly.

"You could get a job on television as a commentator. Or you could write for newspapers, or lecture. Your options are unlimited. You're a celebrity."

"Hardly that." But he looked pleased.

"If the local media knew you were available, they'd be inundating you with offers," she assured him. "You could choose your field."

"It might be a nice change to do lighter stuff for a while," he mused. "Not puff pieces, but stories about local politics and environmental issues."

Jessica could see interest replacing the discontent on his intelligent face. "San Francisco isn't a military zone, but there are plenty of battles that need winning here."

Mrs. Bartlett came in and gazed at them hopefully. "Would it be all right if I cleared the table?"

"Yes, we're finished." After glancing at her watch, Jessica was surprised at how long she and Blade had been talking. "I'm sorry we kept you so late," she apologized.

"No problem." The older woman beamed at them approvingly. "It's nice that you young people have so much to say to each other."

Jessica and Blade left the dining room together, then paused rather awkwardly in the hall. Their unexpected détente left both a little uncomfortable.

"Well...I guess I'll go to my room and finish my book," she said.

"I have some letters to write," he remarked. After a moment's hesitation he said, "Thanks, Jessica. I know you just want to get me out of your hair, but I needed that pep talk. It's time I started putting it all together."

"I'm glad if I helped," she murmured.

"You did. I owe you one." He smiled. "I was only joking about our getting married, but you're going to make some lucky guy a terrific wife."

Jessica went up the stairs with decidedly mixed emotions. Blade could be very charming when he wanted to. Maybe she'd been better off when they were distant to each other.

Enrolling Kevin in school wasn't the most pleasant task she'd ever had. He resisted every step of the way. By the time she left him at school and drove home, Jessica was thoroughly depressed. She was the one who needed encouragement this time. But Blade wasn't home.

"Mr. Dunsmuir went out early this morning," Hawkins informed her. "He said he didn't know when he'd be back."

Jessica knew her disappointment was irrational. Wasn't that what she wanted—to get Blade and Kevin out of the house? Now she could finally get some work done. But her eyes kept straying to the sparkling blue ocean outside.

It was a long dull day, interrupted mainly by telephone calls for Blade. The list was extensive by the time he finally returned in the late afternoon.

"You look busy," he said tentatively, standing in the doorway to the den. Blade brought an air of vitality to the quiet room.

"I can take a break. You seem more cheerful than usual," she remarked. "Did you have a good day?"

"A fantastic day! How about you?"

"It was a little on the quiet side, except for the telephone. I took a stack of messages for you."

"I'm sorry. I'll have a separate phone line and an answering machine installed."

"I wasn't complaining." She stood up and stretched. "I enjoyed the human contact. The solitude around here kind of got to me."

"You need to get out of the house. Put on a jacket and we'll go out for some fresh air."

Jessica's spirits perked up immediately. "That sounds good. I'll be with you in a minute."

While she tidied up her desk, Blade flipped through the messages she'd handed him. His attention sharpened at one of them. "Hmm, Crystal," he murmured.

Jessica wasn't surprised. The name belonged to a throaty female voice that had conjured up visions of a flowing mane of hair and a drop-dead body.

"I'll make a couple of phone calls while you're getting ready," Blade remarked casually.

Jessica had envisioned a walk on the beach. A flight of steps at the back of the house led down to the sand. But when she returned in a windbreaker, he led her to the front door. In the driveway outside was a gleaming white sports car.

"How do you like it?" he asked proudly. "Isn't she a beauty?"

"You bought a new car?"

"I needed wheels to get around."

His father's stately Rolls-Royce sat in the garage, but Jessica understood why Blade didn't care to drive anything that ostentatious.

"It looks like you," she said.

"I'll take that as a compliment." He helped her into the passenger seat. After sliding behind the wheel he said, "How about driving down to Carmel? We can have dinner along the way."

"Mrs. Bartlett has prepared dinner," Jessica said reluctantly. "We have to consider Kevin, too. I don't think he should be left alone tonight. Today must have been rough on him."

Blade turned his head to look at her with a softened expression. "Has anyone ever told you that you're a very nice person? Kevin is my responsibility, but I'm glad to have you on my team."

"For better or worse, we're in this together," she answered, keeping her voice light.

"That's a comforting thought." He put the car into gear and drove through the tree-lined streets of Sea Cliff, looking thoughtful. "I've never depended on anyone before."

"Because you considered it a sign of weakness?"

"I don't think that was the reason. I simply never needed anyone until now. But you changed that." He gave her a radiant smile that warmed Jessica's blood. Until he added, "You're like a wise little sister who straightens me out when I go off course."

"That's another skill I can put in my résumé," she said curtly. "Counseling the confused."

"I'll give you a testimonial. After your motivational talk last night I stopped feeling sorry for myself and decided to get my act together. You're looking at the newest reporter on the *San Francisco Journal.*"

"You have a job?"

He nodded. "I'm really charged up about it, too. I'll be doing in-depth features about the problems facing the city today. My first project is youth gang activity and the problem of infiltration from organized gangs in other cities."

Jessica laughed helplessly. "You're not happy unless you're in a war zone, are you?"

"It's what I know best." He shrugged. "And your war zone analogy is correct. These kids are armed and dangerous. Something has to be done to defuse the situation before they destroy each other.'' He radiated vitality as he talked about other stories he planned to cover.

''You have a busy agenda mapped out,'' she remarked.

''That's what my guidance counselor advised.''

Her face clouded. ''I only hope I can be as successful with Kevin.''

''He'll be okay. Now that he has a stable home environment, Kevin will be a completely different kid.''

''Would you call our living arrangements normal?''

''They could be a lot worse,'' he answered curtly.

Jessica was silent as she gazed at Blade's austere profile. Where was the compassion he'd professed for his nephew? Did Blade really care about anybody but himself? She had a sudden feeling that underneath his surface charm was a very ruthless man. Not too far underneath, either. Then he smiled, and the impression was dispelled.

''At least we all have our own bedrooms,'' he teased. ''Just think if we had to double up.''

''You and Kevin might get to know each other better,'' she replied evenly.

''You and I certainly would.'' Although he was joking, his eyes held a predatory gleam as they swept over her.

''You could scarcely share a room with your little sister,'' she said tartly.

''I'm glad you *aren't* my little sister. I'd cross-examine every guy who came to take you out.''

''Your concern would be misplaced. The men I go out with are interested in more than sex,'' she answered primly.

Blade seemed amused, but his voice was innocent. "They sound like men of high character."

"They are," she assured him.

"I'd be interested in meeting your friends. Perhaps we could double-date some night."

Jessica suspected that Blade was putting her on, but she went along with him. "That sounds as though you intend to resume your social life."

"Your first suggestion was so successful, I decided to take all your advice."

"I'm sure Crystal will be happy about that."

His low chuckle held a distinctly male note. "I hope we both will."

"We'd better go home," Jessica said abruptly. "Mrs. Bartlett has dinner waiting."

Chapter Three

Blade's good mood didn't survive dinner. Kevin was a brooding presence at the table. He seldom raised his eyes from his plate, although he only picked at his food.

When dessert was served he pushed it away and stood up. "I don't want any."

Mrs. Bartlett looked distressed. "I thought all boys liked chocolate cake. Can I get you some ice cream instead?"

"He'll eat what you've prepared, or he'll do without dessert," Blade said evenly.

"It's no trouble," the housekeeper protested.

"I don't want either one," Kevin said with a defiant look at his uncle. "I'm going to my room."

"After you ask to be excused," Blade said.

Their eyes met and held in a clash of strong wills. Jessica held her breath, waiting for an eruption from one or both. Blade's gray eyes were steely, and Kevin's jaw was thrust out pugnaciously. The family resemblance between them was very visible at that instant.

After a nerve-stretching moment Kevin backed down. "May I be excused?" he muttered.

When the child had left the room Jessica said, "Was that really necessary? Did you have to challenge him like that?"

"No. I could let him go on being rude and self-centered, but I wouldn't be doing him a favor. He has to learn to live with other people."

"I know, but sometimes I'm afraid we're fighting a losing battle." She sighed. "Do you think he'll ever be a normal little boy again?"

"Sooner than you imagine. He'll stop acting like a brat when he finds out he can't get away with it. Your problem is you worry too much. You need to get out, maybe see a good movie."

Jessica brightened. "I'd like that. A comedy, preferably. I haven't seen a movie in ages, so anything you choose will be fine."

"Oh... well, I didn't mean..." He looked uncomfortable. "Actually I'm tied up tonight, but I'd be delighted to take you tomorrow night."

Her cheeks flamed with embarrassment. She should have realized he was only offering advice. "I was asking for a recommendation," she covered up hastily. "I didn't expect you to go with me."

"I'd like to very much," he said gently. "Are we on for tomorrow night?"

"I already have a date," she answered coolly. "Maybe some other time."

Jessica didn't really have a date, but she was determined to make one before the following evening. After dinner she went into the den to make some phone calls.

Unfortunately, all the men she enjoyed going out with were unavailable. She was finally forced to settle for Henry, a man she'd dated occasionally, mainly because he was so persistent.

"This is the first time you ever called me." Wonder filled his voice. "I've had such trouble getting a date with you that I was beginning to think you didn't want to go out with me."

"I've been awfully busy lately, moving and all. You know how it is." Jessica had the grace to feel slightly ashamed of using him, but this was an emergency.

"I'm glad you're finally settled. How does it feel to live in a mansion?"

"I could get used to it."

"Enjoy it while you can. Those big old houses will all be torn down soon."

"What makes you think so?"

"Investment-wise, single-family homes that size are a terrible misuse of capital. Do you realize what that much money invested, even cautiously, would bring?"

"No," she murmured.

"Plenty, believe me! Not to mention the tax advantages. Those alone would be substantial."

Jessica suppressed a sigh. Was her pride really worth an evening of this? "I'm sure you're right, Henry, but—" A sudden uproar outside the den startled her. "I have to go. Something's come up. I'll see you tomorrow night."

She rushed into the hall to find Blade shouting for Kevin, his eyes glittering with rage. "If I have to come up there and get you, you'll be in worse trouble than you are now!"

"What on earth happened?" Jessica asked.

"That little monster let the air out of my tires!"

Her first impulse was to laugh, but she knew better. Blade's body was as taut as a tiger's on a leash, and his features appeared chiseled out of stone.

"What makes you think Kevin did it?" she asked, struggling to keep a straight face. "Maybe you picked up a nail."

"In all four tires? Kevin!"

The boy came down the stairs slowly. Apprehension was apparent in every movement, but deep in his eyes was a glint of satisfaction.

"I'll give you one minute to explain yourself," Blade thundered. "Did you honestly think you could get away with this vandalism? I've seen irresponsible kids in my day, but you're the absolute limit!"

"Give him a chance to talk," Jessica murmured. "Did you let the air out of your uncle's tires, Kevin?"

"Yes." His answer was barely audible, but he didn't attempt to lie.

"If you expect me to put up with this behavior, you're sadly mistaken, young man," Blade stormed.

Kevin shrugged slightly. "So send me back to boarding school."

"I'm tempted to send you to outer Mongolia," Blade muttered. "Go to your room and stay there."

"For how long?" Kevin was clearly testing his uncle's limits.

"I might possibly allow you out to vote when you're twenty-one, but don't count on it." After Kevin had gone back upstairs, Blade tried to contain his anger. "I'm going to walk up to the gas station and see what they can do. I don't have time to wait for the auto club."

"Can I drive you to the station?" Jessica asked.

"No, I need to walk off some steam. You can do me a favor, though. Call Crystal Hansen and tell her I'll be delayed."

Mrs. Bartlett had been drawn to the hall by the commotion. After he left she said, "Mr. Blade hasn't lost that healthy temper, I see. Luckily he'll be all over it by morning."

"Maybe, but I hope Kevin will have sense enough to walk softly around him for a while. You really can't blame Blade for being angry."

The older woman chuckled unexpectedly. "I knew that boy was a real Dunsmuir. Mr. Blade chooses not to remember, but he and his brother used to pull the same kind of stunts on each other. This place was really lively when they were young."

"It will be again if I don't call his date and tell her he'll be late."

"She'll wait," Mrs. Bartlett said complacently. "He could always wrap the ladies around his little finger."

The knowledge that she was probably right annoyed Jessica. A tiny smile tilted her lips as she decided to make Blade's job a little more difficult this time.

Her voice dropped to a sexy register when Crystal answered the phone. "I'm calling for Blade Dunsmuir, Miss Hansen. He asked me to tell you he's been unavoidably detained."

"Who is this?" Crystal asked sharply.

"Just a friend of Blade."

"Exactly what detained him?"

Jessica laughed throatily. "Something completely unforeseen. He couldn't help himself, I promise you."

There was a short silence at the other end of the line. Then Crystal asked, "How late will he be?"

"That's hard to say, but he'll be over as soon as everything gets back to normal."

"Let me speak to him," Crystal said ominously.

"He isn't here right now. He said he had to go out to cool off. Shall I have him phone you before he comes over?"

"Don't bother. Tell him I'll pick *him* up."

Jessica cradled the receiver with a satisfied expression. She hadn't said anything that wasn't true, had she? If Crystal wanted to leap to conclusions, that was her problem. Jessica was about to retreat to the safety of her room when Blade returned.

"Did you call Crystal?" he asked.

"Yes. She's coming over here, so you don't have to rush."

"That was thoughtful of her."

"Very. Well...have a good time."

As she started for the door, Blade stopped her. "Do you think I was too hard on Kevin?"

"No, you couldn't let him get away with it. He didn't do any real damage, though. He wasn't being malicious, just striking back."

Blade smiled ruefully. "I can't help admiring the kid's spunk. It's something I might have done at his age."

"So Mrs. Bartlett told me. She indicated you and your brother were a couple of demons."

His face held remembrance. "She could tell you some stories. I don't know how our parents put up with us."

"The same way we'll cope with Kevin."

"That's all very well for you to say. He didn't let the air out of *your* tires."

"I didn't make him toe the line."

"So you do think I came on too strong."

"No, somebody had to take a stand. I'm just glad it was you."

"I don't *enjoy* being the heavy," he complained.

"But you do it so well," Jessica teased. "I've never seen smoke come out of anyone's nostrils before."

"As you've seen, I'm all bark and no bite."

"I'm not so sure." She looked at him appraisingly. Blade could be intimidating in more ways than one.

He laughed, taking her hand and guiding it to his head. "Feel for yourself. Not a single horn."

Jessica enjoyed the sensuous sensation of running her fingers through his thick hair. She unconsciously prolonged the pleasure, gazing up into his sparkling eyes. At that precise moment Mrs. Bartlett ushered a beautiful brunette woman into the den.

"I guess you didn't hear the doorbell," the housekeeper remarked, not helping matters.

"Crystal, how good of you to drive over." Blade gave her a welcoming smile. "I really got myself into a situation here."

"That's the impression I got." Her narrowed eyes raked Jessica before returning to Blade. "You really should schedule your women farther apart."

"What kind of remark is that?" he asked with a puzzled frown. "I'm sorry about the mix-up tonight, but it had nothing to do with Jessica. We're merely friends."

"Actually I'm more like Blade's little sister," Jessica said with a demure glance at him.

He grinned. "I meant it as a compliment, but I have a feeling I'm going to pay dearly for that remark."

Crystal gritted her even white teeth at the shared intimacy between them. "Am I wrong, or do we have a date tonight, Blade?"

Jessica hadn't cared for Crystal on the phone, and she liked her even less in person. She had no compunction about adding to the woman's misconception.

"I'm sorry if I've held you up," she apologized. "I'll go to my room now. See you in the morning, Blade."

"She's staying here?" Crystal asked him.

Jessica answered before he could. "Oh, dear. Didn't Blade tell you we're living together?"

"No, it apparently slipped his mind."

"We aren't exactly living together." Blade shot Jessica a look of annoyance.

"Either you are or you aren't," Crystal snapped. "I'd like to know what's going on around here."

"It's all rather complicated." Blade sighed.

"Simplify it," she said tersely. "Starting with the reason you were delayed tonight."

"Didn't Jessica tell you what happened?"

"I didn't go into details." Jessica edged toward the door.

"You seem to have said plenty." Blade gazed at her impassively.

"Well, I'm sure you can straighten everything out." She thought it prudent to leave.

On thinking it over, Jessica rather regretted sabotaging Blade's evening, although Crystal wouldn't be any great loss. She might be sexy, but the woman had the personality of a tarantula. Blade obviously had a different opinion, though, and if he couldn't patch things up, he was apt to be very vocal about his displeasure.

She needn't have worried, at least about Blade's powers of persuasion. A creaking board in the upstairs hall woke Jessica when he returned home. Her bedside clock showed it was after three in the morning.

* * *

In spite of his late night, Blade showed up for breakfast, an event Jessica could have foregone. She waited defensively for a tirade that didn't come. Kevin shared her concern, but Blade's forgiveness included him.

"One of the nice things about our arrangement is having breakfast together," he remarked pleasantly. "I never did like to eat alone."

"It isn't much fun," Jessica agreed neutrally.

"That's one of the benefits of living with someone. Of course there are also liabilities."

After a wary glance at him she said, "Would you like more toast, Kevin?"

"No, thank you." He was chastened enough to be polite without being prompted. "I'm all done. Can I go now?"

"Yes," Jessica said reluctantly. She wasn't anxious to be alone with Blade.

A small silence fell in the room, but only Jessica was uncomfortable. Blade ate his pancakes with calm enjoyment.

While she was casting about for a safe topic of conversation, he said, "Did you have any reason for giving Crystal the impression that you and I were having a torrid affair?"

"I never did any such thing!"

"Shall I repeat a few of the things you told her?"

"They were all true. It's not my fault if she misinterpreted them. You might try dating women with higher IQs."

He looked amused. "If I want to discuss global politics, I can have a conversation with my barber."

"It's nice to know what you consider important in a woman," Jessica remarked witheringly.

"Now *you're* the one laboring under a misapprehension. I am not a male chauvinist. I enjoy the company of women for a variety of reasons. Unlike you, I don't discriminate against the ones who are beautiful."

"That's very broad-minded of you. I suppose you were discussing the greenhouse effect and the ozone layer until three in the morning."

He raised a sardonic eyebrow. "If I'd known you were waiting up for me, I would have stopped by."

Jessica's cheeks flamed at her inadvertent admission. "Don't be ridiculous! A board in the hall squeaks, and I'm a very light sleeper."

"We must have it fixed. I wouldn't want to be responsible for causing you any sleepless nights."

"I appreciate your concern," she said dryly.

He gave her a broad smile. "You're going to see more of it."

Jessica wasn't sure what he meant by that, but she was happy to have gotten off so lightly. Blade could have made her life miserable, yet he wasn't holding a grudge. She resolved to stay out of his affairs in the future.

Jessica dressed for her date that night with a marked lack of enthusiasm. Why hadn't she accepted Blade's invitation to the movies instead? In spite of the occasional friction between them, he was stimulating company. It would have been a pleasant evening. What difference did it make if he thought she couldn't get another date? Those were the games people played when they were romantically involved, which she and Blade weren't. They had enough problems without adding that one.

She couldn't help wondering—intellectually, of course—what kind of lover he would be. Physically, Blade was everything any woman could want, and an impressive number did. Was he tender and unhurried, though? Did he build the mood with tantalizing kisses and caresses, seeking out all the erotic pleasure spots, inspiring his partner to do the same? His powerful body must be terribly impressive in the nude.

Jessica's breath caught in her throat as she realized how vivid her speculation had become. What on earth had gotten into her? She was acting like a teenager first discovering sex.

Jessica would have preferred not to see Blade at the moment, but he called to her from the den when she went downstairs.

The room looked very cozy with a fire crackling in the fireplace and all the lamps lit. The book-lined shelves glowed with color, along with the richly patterned Oriental rug.

"I hope you don't mind my sitting in here," he said. "The living room feels so formal."

"It's your house. You can go wherever you like," Jessica answered, more curtly than she meant to.

"You use this room as an office, though."

"I'm happy to share it," she said, to make amends. "Aren't you going out tonight?"

"I don't have any plans."

If he was trying to make her feel sorry for him, he hadn't succeeded. Jessica knew Blade could find many forms of entertainment if he wanted to.

"It's nice to have a free night every now and then," she remarked as the doorbell rang. "Have a pleasant evening."

Henry stood on the doorstep with a bunch of flowers in his hand. "For you," he said unnecessarily.

His intentions were good, but Jessica was annoyed rather than pleased. She'd intended to hustle Henry out the door before Blade could meet him. Now she'd have to go in the kitchen for a vase.

"How thoughtful," she said with a forced smile. "But you shouldn't have."

"It was a big event when you phoned me for a date. I thought it called for something special."

"I'll put these in water. Stay right here," she ordered. "It will only take a minute."

It took longer than that because she couldn't find a vase. Finally she stuffed the bouquet into a water pitcher and dashed back to the hall. Too late, as it turned out. Blade was leading Henry into the den.

"I'm back," she announced. "We can go now."

"Henry just accepted my offer of a drink," Blade said. "We introduced ourselves."

"We don't have time for a drink," she answered. "We're going to a movie."

"It doesn't start for forty minutes," Henry said reassuringly.

"But we have to get there and park."

"The parking lot is right next door."

"If I didn't know better, I'd think you didn't want Henry and me to get acquainted," Blade commented innocently. "But that couldn't be. We had such a fun time when you met *my* friend, Crystal."

So much for not holding a grudge, Jessica thought grimly. How did Blade plan to retaliate?

"This is certainly a nice house you have here," Henry remarked, glancing around. "Do you plan on keeping it?"

"I'm sure Blade has excellent financial advice," Jessica said hastily.

"It's always good to get another opinion," Blade observed. "Are you in the real estate business, Henry?"

"No, I'm a CPA with the largest accounting firm in San Francisco—Peabody, Carstairs and Strathmore."

"I'm impressed," Blade murmured.

"You should be," Jessica said sharply. "Accountants are highly trained professionals. I'll bet you couldn't make out your own tax return."

"You're so right," Blade agreed readily. "I have great respect for people who can make sense out of government forms. I'm at a complete loss when the instructions tell me to add line A to line B, unless the total is more than the sum of lines three and four."

Henry chuckled indulgently. "Don't feel badly. I couldn't be a foreign correspondent."

"It's somewhat similar. We both deal in human misery."

"I'll have to tell that to the guys around the office. Maybe we should put in for combat pay."

"Why not? Facing a tax audit must be a perilous experience."

Jessica was getting angrier by the minute, although she couldn't decide which one of them aggravated her more, Blade for being so snide, or Henry for being such a wimp.

"We have to leave," she declared. "I don't want to miss the start of the movie."

"What are you going to see?" Blade asked.

"*Bread and Hollyhocks*," Henry answered. "It's a new Swedish film. The review in the *Post* showed a little man applauding. That means the critic liked it, so I figure it must be good."

"No sense making your own choice and being disappointed," Blade agreed. "I've been wanting to see that movie myself. Maybe I'll catch it tonight, since I don't have anything else to do."

"If we're all going to the same show, you might as well come with us," Henry said. "It would be foolish to take two cars."

"That's awfully generous of you. Are you sure I won't be intruding?"

"How can you even ask such a thing?" Jessica demanded in outrage.

"Does that mean I would be, or I wouldn't?" Blade asked.

"Of course you would! I can't believe you'd have the audacity to horn in on someone else's date."

"Uh-oh! I'm really going to catch it later." Blade winked at the other man.

Henry attempted to make peace. "I did ask him, Jess."

"Anyone with a grain of sensitivity would have refused," she stormed.

Blade began to chuckle. "She's right, I've been a clod. Jessica's been looking forward to this date all day. Every other word was Henry this and Henry that."

"Really?" A pleased expression dawned on his face. "I never would have guessed."

"Women don't like men to know their opinion of them. And believe me, Henry, you're one of the men she's been keeping it from."

When Henry turned dazzled eyes on her, Jessica snapped, "Oh, for heaven's sake, don't you know when you're being had? You ought to be ashamed of yourself, Blade!"

"There's such a thing as playing *too* hard to get," he chided gently. "You don't want Henry to get discouraged."

"No fear of that," the other man declared. "I plan to be a permanent fixture around here from now on."

"You see what a little honesty will do?" Blade asked her.

"I won't forget this," she said grimly.

"No need to thank me. Just knowing what I've done is reward enough. You two lovebirds run along. I've kept you apart long enough."

"I'll get even with you if it's the last thing I do," she muttered.

Blade smiled dangerously. "If I were you, I'd settle for a draw."

Jessica was seething with a desire to lash out at everyone in sight, when Kevin called to her from the stairs. He got the fallout from her wrath.

"What is it?" she asked tersely, stalking into the hall.

"The teacher gave me a paper for you to sign. It's so I can go on a field trip to the museum tomorrow."

"She gave it to you just today? That's pretty short notice."

"Well, maybe it was a few days ago. But I have to hand it in tomorrow."

"All right, give it to me." When he handed her the sheet of paper she said, "Didn't you bring a pen?"

He shrugged. "I thought you'd have one."

"Only during working hours. As of now, I'm supposed to be on my own time." Jessica was conscious of the men's voices in the den. What further pitfalls was Blade digging for her? She gave the paper back to Kevin. "Give this to your uncle. He should be the one to sign it, anyway."

The boy's lower lip jutted out. "I don't want anything to do with him."

"Join the club, pal. But you'll have to suffer like all the rest of us."

She had a moment's compunction over her curt tone, but not at sending him to his uncle. Blade would be pleasant to him, and the enforced communication might be an icebreaker between the two.

She dismissed Kevin's problems in favor of her own. Henry was holding forth about tax shelters and fiduciary responsibility. He continued to expound even after she joined them.

"That's really fascinating," Blade said finally. "You'll have to tell me more sometime, but right now I think Jessica is getting impatient."

"I crossed over into homicidal long ago," she stated.

Blade grinned. "Have a good time, and don't do anything I wouldn't do."

The tired cliché was so patently phony that Jessica simply gave him a disgusted look and left without answering.

She hadn't expected much from the evening even before Blade's interference, and her fears were justified. Even the movie was boring. Jessica couldn't wait to get home, but Henry insisted on going somewhere to eat first.

"The least I can do is buy you a hamburger, since you wouldn't let me take you out to dinner," he said.

"Blade and I sort of agreed to have dinner at home with Kevin for a couple of weeks. We don't like to leave him until he feels more secure."

"If I didn't know Blade was on my side, I'd be jealous of all the time you spend with him."

"He's the *last* man in the world you'd have reason to be jealous of."

"Don't be angry at him for letting the cat out of the bag. I'm flattered." He tried to take her hand across the table, and succeeded in getting catsup on his fingers instead. "It sure was lucky for me that I got to meet Blade."

"Believe me, luck had nothing to do with it."

"You mean it was fate or something?"

"Or something. Wipe your fingers, Henry. You look like you're bleeding."

A light showed under Blade's bedroom door when Jessica finally got home. It was the room across from hers. She was tempted to barge in and tell him what she thought of him, then decided against it. That was probably what he expected. A cool dismissal of the entire incident would be more dignified.

Living with Kevin and Blade was like living in an amusement park fun house, Jessica reflected as she got undressed. You never knew what was going to happen next. Her mouth curved suddenly as she remembered how irate Blade had been over his car, and how funny it had struck her. Had she overreacted just as badly over something equally trivial? Well, at least she wasn't alone. They both had quick tempers.

She decided to drop any plans for revenge. Much as she hated to let Blade get away with his prank, she had to admit he was justified. She'd put him in as bad a spot with Crystal. Besides, he was a formidable adversary. Jessica had a feeling Blade was a lot trickier than she could ever be.

After brushing her teeth, she put on a seafoam-green chiffon nightgown. Beautiful lingerie was one of her private indulgences. She loved the feeling of silk and satin against her bare skin, and this was her favorite gown. By the time she was ready for bed, her good humor was completely restored.

A single lamp illuminated the pale pink pillows and matching blanket cover. Jessica pulled back the top sheet, then let out a piercing shriek. Something long and black was coiled between the sheets. She cringed away, unable to stop screaming.

The door flew open, and Blade dashed in wearing only navy silk pajama bottoms. He raced over and took her in his arms. "What happened? Are you all right?"

She clung to him like a drowning woman, wrapping her arms around his torso and pressing so closely against him that his hard thigh muscles bruised her legs.

"Did someone get into your room?" He tried to loosen her arms, but she held on convulsively. "Answer me, Jessica! What's wrong?"

"It was a snake." Her words were muffled against his bare chest.

"I can't hear you." He lifted her chin.

"I saw a snake."

His anxiety disappeared, and he stroked her hair gently. "You were dreaming, honey."

"No, I saw it! It's in my bed."

He disengaged her arms and glanced around fruitlessly for a club of some kind. "Do you have an umbrella?" he asked finally.

"In the closet," she whispered.

As Blade approached the bed with his makeshift weapon, Jessica watched in horrified fascination. She cowered when he raised his arm, then almost fainted when he picked up the horrid thing on the sheet.

"I can see why this would scare the wits out of you," he said, walking toward her.

She backed away. "Are you out of your mind? You'll get bitten."

"Not by this—it's plastic. Kevin strikes again." Blade chuckled.

"I don't believe it! That little villain put a fake snake in my bed?"

"He wasn't being malicious, just striking back." He mimicked her earlier words with a wide grin.

"What he did to you was a childish prank. This is a . . . an outrage! I'm still shaking."

Blade's amusement changed to male awareness as his interested gaze traveled over her skimpily clad body. "Yes, I could see you were upset," he murmured.

Jessica felt herself growing warm as she remembered the way she'd attached herself to him like a leech. Since she was now acquainted with every taut muscle and tendon in his rangy body, he must have equal knowledge of her own anatomy. And what he hadn't felt, he could see. She folded her arms over her breasts in an effort at concealment, but that left other areas vulnerable.

"I'm all right now." She avoided his eyes. "You can go back to sleep."

"I was reading. And neither of us will be able to get to sleep for a while. Why don't we go down to the kitchen for some hot chocolate?"

"I really don't want any."

"It will do you good," he coaxed.

She gave in. Anything to get him out of her room! "Okay, I'll meet you there in a couple of minutes."

Jessica felt a lot better after she put on a peach-colored satin caftan with lace ruffles around the neck and wrists. The voluminous folds concealed all evidence of the curved body underneath.

Blade had put on a robe, too, she was relieved to see. It covered the pajama pants that rode low on his narrow hips in the kind of centerfold effect found in certain

women's magazines. His suggestively tousled hair was the
only reminder of that playboy image.

Jessica couldn't help feeling a little uncomfortable with
him, but Blade's casual attitude soon put her at ease. The
flash of sexual awareness that had ignited between them
might never have happened. He was getting milk from
the refrigerator as though it were the most normal thing
in the world to be having hot chocolate together in the
middle of the night.

"How about a sandwich?" he asked. "I see some ham
and cheese that look good."

"Not for me, but I'll fix you one. I just had a hamburger."

"I wondered what kept you."

"I'm surprised you expected me home at all after you
delivered me to Henry gift wrapped."

"He's not your type."

"How do you know what my type is?" She spread
mustard on a slice of bread and layered on ham and
cheese.

"It would have to be someone more intellectually
stimulating."

"I would have said the same about you until I met
Crystal."

Blade smiled. "You have to go through a lot of Crys-
tals and Henrys before you find true love."

"Is that what you're looking for?" she asked curiously.

"Isn't everybody?"

"Most people, but you're different," she said slowly.

"In what way?"

"You're so self-sufficient. You don't seem to need
anybody."

"Nobody chooses to go it alone. If I seem like a loner it's because I haven't found my other half. I still have hopes, though."

Jessica sat down opposite him at the kitchen table. "What will she be like?"

"Someone warm and generous, with a lively mind and a sense of humor."

"Does she have to be beautiful?"

"She will be to me. But most of all she'll love me for myself, not my money." His bemused expression hardened. "People do incredible things for money."

Blade was in a position to know, Jessica thought sadly. He'd given up his career for it. But who was she to judge? Hadn't she also made concessions?

"I guess when you're very rich you tend to question people's motives," she agreed soberly.

His smile was twisted. "The ancient Romans coined a phrase for that kind of dilemma. *Est nullus prandium libero.* Which translates to, there's no free lunch."

Chapter Four

Kevin usually had to be summoned to breakfast several times before he put in a grudging appearance. The morning after the snake incident, however, he was the first one downstairs. His obvious intention was to skip breakfast entirely and leave the house without having to see Jessica or Blade.

Jessica foiled this plan. She'd spent a restless night, in spite of the hot chocolate that was supposed to relax her. The brief physical encounter with Blade had been of no importance, but her subconscious mind had dwelt on the incident. In her dreams, she was in his arms once more, only this time it wasn't accidentally.

She was a willing participant in the erotic fantasy. As Blade's scorching mouth trailed down her neck to the hidden valley between her breasts, she slowly untied the strings of his pajama bottoms. The soft fabric slithered down his hips, followed by her caressing hands, eager to experience him fully. Blade's hoarse cry of exultation was still sounding in her ears as she awoke with a start.

Jessica was appalled at the dream, and even more at herself for a brief flash of regret that it had ended too soon. What was it about Blade that produced such strange reactions in her? She didn't even *like* him a good part of the time!

Much later she'd drifted back into a fitful sleep, only to awaken at dawn. This time she got up and dressed, relieved to see the night end.

Kevin was headed for the front door when Jessica reached the foot of the stairs. "Where are you going so early?" she called.

"To school." He gave her an uneasy look.

"At this hour? It's only seven o'clock. Have you had breakfast already?"

He hesitated. "No. Mrs. Bartlett isn't down yet."

"I'll make breakfast for you," she offered.

"I'm not hungry." He edged toward the door.

"You have to eat something. Besides, I want to talk to you."

"Okay." He gave up trying to escape, and heaved an exaggerated sigh. "Go ahead and yell at me."

"Come in the kitchen. I need coffee before I can even talk, let alone yell."

Jessica smothered a smile as he followed her with all the enthusiasm of a dog about to be bathed. While filling the coffee maker, she asked, "What would you like to eat?"

He shrugged. "I don't care."

She gazed at him judiciously. "I could make scrambled eggs and put a lot of hot pepper sauce in them. But that would start a whole new round of practical jokes. You'd feel the need to get even with me, and then I'd have to do the same to you. Is that what you really want?"

He looked at her defiantly. "I suppose you want me to say I'm sorry I put that snake in your bed."

"Would you say it if I told you to?"

"I guess so."

"That surprises me, because one thing I've learned about you is that you don't lie."

"Well, maybe I'm sorry now," he mumbled.

"I am, too—sorry that I was sharp with you last night. I was angry at someone else, and I shouldn't have taken it out on you."

"That's okay," he answered awkwardly.

"No, it isn't, but it might happen again because people who live together are sometimes thoughtless to each other. I just want you to know I didn't mean to be. I'd like to be your friend, Kevin."

"Why? You don't really like me. Nobody does." He lowered his head to hide the tears that threatened.

"That's not true. Everybody in this house wants to make you happy, but you won't let us. We want to be your family."

"You can't be. My family is dead and buried, and I wish I was, too!"

He stood up, prepared to make his usual dash out the door, but Jessica blocked the way. "I know how you feel, whether you believe it or not. I don't have any parents, either. They didn't die as tragically as yours did, but I thought they were the only two people in the world who truly cared about me. I know what it's like to be scared and lonely."

"You're a grown-up," he said uncertainly.

"That's no magic key to happiness." Jessica smiled. "Sometimes the only advantage to being an adult is you get to stay up as late as you like. We need love and affection the same as you do."

"I don't need anybody." He scowled.

"If you were truly self-sufficient, you'd be a happier young man. You can't keep fighting the whole world, Kevin. You have to trust somebody. Your parents would be sad to see you so miserable."

His face crumpled suddenly and tears streamed out of his eyes. "I didn't even get to say goodbye to them. I was at summer camp, and they were coming up for parents' day."

Jessica folded him in her arms as sobs racked his thin body. "Just remember how happy you were when you were together. You'll always have wonderful memories of the good times you shared. Don't let regrets spoil those."

"Why did they have to die?" His tortured words were muffled against her shoulder.

She smoothed his hair tenderly. "I wish I could answer that, but I can't. A lot of things seem unfair, yet there's nothing we can do about it. You have to pick up the pieces of your own life and go on, the way they would have wanted."

His sobs had died to an occasional hiccup, but he continued to cling to her. "Will you help me?"

The lump in Jessica's throat felt like a watermelon. "You bet I will! From now on I'm your official problem-solver."

Kevin drew away hurriedly at the sound of footsteps in the hall. He turned his back to hide the recent tears when he saw his uncle.

Not understanding the child's reason, Blade's gray eyes darkened. "What crisis are we having this morning?" he asked Jessica.

"What makes you think there is one?"

"Just the usual—your pink cheeks and sullen Sam over there."

"Don't call him that!" she flared. "If you can't be civil, get out of this kitchen."

"It happens to be *my* kitchen."

"All right, then we'll leave. Come on, Kevin, I'll take you out to breakfast."

"Wait a minute." Blade's hand clamped around her wrist. "Will you kindly tell me what's going on? Last night you were ready to skin the kid alive, and this morning *I'm* the villain."

"I might have overreacted a little last night, but I didn't mean anything by it."

His annoyed expression changed to a mocking smile. "I'm sorry to hear that. Your metamorphosis into a clinging vine was most enjoyable."

The color in Jessica's cheeks deepened. "I was frightened out of my wits. Anyone who took a good look at me could see that."

He grinned broadly. "The glimpse I caught made me want to see more."

Blade had her at a disadvantage. This was no time to argue with him. Not while she was trying to convince Kevin that his uncle was really one of the good guys.

Biting her lip over the dilemma, she murmured, "Please, Blade, I'd prefer to drop the whole thing. Kevin and I straightened everything out." She put her arm around the boy's shoulders.

Blade stared at him with a raised eyebrow. "You must make one hell of an apology. Care to share your secret with me?"

"Don't do it, Kevin," Jessica advised. "He'll just use it to flimflam some gullible female."

"Would I do a thing like that?" Blade appealed to him.

Kevin smiled tentatively, slightly dazed at being included as an equal in their easy exchange. "I don't know. Maybe you would."

"You and I need to have a long talk, chum," Blade said. "In the battle of the sexes, we males have to stick together. Women already have the advantage."

"Because we're smarter?" Jessica asked smugly.

He gave her a melting smile. "No, because you've convinced us we can't live without you."

"How hard have you tried?" she asked dryly.

"It would be wasted effort. One glimpse of a green chiffon nightie, and all my willpower would vanish."

Jessica gave him an annoyed look. Blade knew she wouldn't rise to the bait in front of his nephew. She glanced at the clock. "It's getting late. Will you set the table, Kevin, while I make breakfast?"

Mrs. Bartlett bustled in before she could begin. "My goodness, you three are early birds. Is something special happening today?"

Blade's eyes glinted with amusement. "I hope not. I'm still recovering from last night."

"What happened?" The housekeeper looked alarmed. "I didn't hear anything."

"Nothing happened," Jessica answered firmly.

"More's the pity," he murmured.

The older woman's face relaxed. "Mr. Blade is always teasing me."

"He's a regular barrel of laughs," Jessica muttered.

The scene around the breakfast table was radically different from the other meals they'd shared. Kevin didn't automatically turn into a carefree, well-adjusted child. That would have been too much to expect. He showed a definite improvement, however. His sullen attitude was replaced by a groping effort at communication.

Very wisely, Jessica didn't try to rush him. She and Blade made him part of the conversation but not the focus of it.

"Did you have a chance to ask your uncle to sign that consent form so you can go to the museum?" she asked casually when they were almost through eating.

"No." Kevin looked uncomfortable at being reminded of the previous night.

"What museum are you going to?" Blade asked.

"The DeYoung."

"That's right across from the Aquarium. Take a look at the flashlight fish if you have a chance. They're really nifty," Blade said.

"I think we have to stay with the class."

"Why don't I take you on Sunday then?"

"Well..." Kevin looked at Jessica beseechingly. He was still defensive with his uncle.

"Maybe Jessica will join us," Blade remarked casually. "We could have a picnic in the park first and make a day of it."

"That sounds like fun." She accepted quickly. "I haven't done either of those things in a long time."

"Are we on for Sunday?" Blade asked his nephew.

"Okay." Kevin gulped his milk down. "I have to go."

After he'd left, Blade looked at Jessica and shook his head. "I always knew you were a siren, but I didn't know you were a sorceress as well. How did you change a sulky brat into a normal kid?"

"He was never a brat," she said reprovingly. "Just a very troubled child. And he isn't out of the woods yet. You'll have to control your temper around him."

"I will if you will." Blade grinned. "He didn't put that snake in your bed for no good reason."

"We both have to make an effort," she admitted. "I'm so glad you suggested spending the day together."

His eyes wandered over her vibrant face. "I'm glad you're going to be there, too."

He only meant her presence would make things easier, but Jessica felt a glow of satisfaction. It was very gratifying to know this self-sufficient man needed her.

On Sunday Mrs. Bartlett packed them a picnic basket and they drove to a lovely meadow in the park. Kevin was very subdued in the back seat of Blade's sports car.

"Do you have enough room?" Jessica asked him. "I don't know why they bothered to put a back seat in this thing. A large dog would have to hang his head out of one window and his tail out the other."

"I didn't buy the car with the intention of hauling dumb animals around," Blade replied.

"Not the four-footed kind, at least," she remarked dryly.

He ignored the barb, looking thoughtful. "Maybe we *should* have a dog. Would you like that, Kevin?"

"Gee, yeah! Could we?" The little boy's face became animated.

"I don't see why not."

"Can we go get him now?" Kevin asked eagerly.

"If we do that we'll have to skip the Aquarium."

"We can go some other time. Please, Uncle Blade!"

Jessica and Blade exchanged a charged glance at this new breakthrough. It was the first time Kevin had ever referred to his uncle by any designation other than "he" or "him."

Blade had to clear his throat before he could answer. "I'll tell you what. Mrs. Bartlett's feelings would be hurt if we didn't eat the lunch she made us. So suppose we have our picnic first, and then we'll go look at puppies."

Kevin agreed reluctantly, and they proceeded with the first part of their original plan. While Jessica and Blade spread a checkered tablecloth on the grass and unpacked the hamper, Kevin made friends with the many dogs that frolicked in the park.

"That was an inspired idea you had," Jessica told him.

"Maybe I'm buying his approval, but I don't care." Blade's voice was husky. "It's worth it to see him smile for a change."

"He would have accepted you anyway. You simply hurried things along." She covered his hand impulsively. "No boy could have a better role model than you."

He turned his hand palm up and clasped it around hers. "This is shaping up to be a red-letter day. Your approval is almost as tough to win as Kevin's."

"That never seemed to bother you," she said lightly.

He stroked the soft skin of her wrist with his forefinger. "Is that what you think?"

She snatched her hand away as her skin started to tingle. "I think my first opinion of you was correct. You can't help coming on to whichever woman you're with, whether you're interested in her or not."

"Dear little Jessica." He looked amused. "Do you honestly think I'd come on to you in a public park with a ten-year-old boy along?" He tipped her chin up and gazed into her stormy eyes. "If I were trying to seduce you, it would be someplace romantic, perhaps a secluded moonlit garden where I could kiss every secret part of you."

As she was staring at him, bemused, Kevin returned to ask plaintively, "Aren't we ever going to eat? The pet store will be closed before we get there."

"I seriously doubt it," Blade assured him. "Let's see what culinary delights Mrs. B. whipped up for us."

Jessica helped silently as he unwrapped sandwiches and opened cans of soft drinks. The way Blade changed emotional gears never failed to irritate her. One minute he was creating a romantic mood that would make any woman's pulse beat faster, and the next minute he was clowning around. It was something to remember in case she was ever tempted to believe the compliments he tossed around when it served his purpose.

Kevin wolfed down his own lunch, and urged them to do the same.

"It took Mrs. Bartlett longer to make this than it's taking us to eat it," Blade complained, but he understood the child's impatience.

On the way to the pet shop in the mall Blade said, "We've neglected to discuss one very important matter. This is your dog, Kevin. You'll be expected to take care of him."

"Oh, I will!" the youngster promised fervently. "I'll even pay for his food out of my allowance."

Blade hid a smile. "That won't be necessary. I'm more interested in seeing you develop a sense of responsibility. This animal will be dependent on you, so you mustn't let him down."

Jessica's feelings toward Blade veered again. He could so easily have overindulged Kevin, assuring the child's approval of him. But Blade had his nephew's welfare at heart, not his own. He'd struck the correct balance between generosity and common sense. It was too bad he didn't have any children of his own. Blade would make a wonderful father, she thought, a trifle wistfully.

The difficulty of choosing a puppy from dozens of equally appealing ones was agonizing. Kevin cuddled small wriggling bodies with bright eyes and pink tongues. He made up his mind, then changed it several times.

Blade didn't try to rush him. He merely smiled indulgently at the youngster's dilemma. Jessica could only sympathize. She wanted to take them all home, too. Finally Kevin decided on an adorable bundle of black and white curly fur.

"This is the one," he declared.

"Are you sure? That's an English sheepdog. He'll be enormous when he grows up," Blade warned. "Besides that, you'll have to brush him every day."

"I don't care. I want him."

"I might have to trade in the sports car," Blade observed wryly to Jessica.

"That's what happens when you get to be a family man," she teased.

"Would you still respect me if I drove a four-door sedan?"

"*I* would, but I don't know about Crystal."

Blade chuckled. "I'd just have to think of some way to make it up to her."

"That shouldn't tax your ingenuity too much," she answered coolly. "Let's take Kevin's dog home while it's still a puppy."

After much deliberation, Kevin decided on the name King, which was fitting. The small ball of fur took over the household and had everyone waiting on him. Mrs. Bartlett filled his bowl with water, Hawkins transformed a wicker basket into a bed, and the other three took him for a romp on the beach. When the puppy flopped down in the sand, completely tuckered out, they carried him into the den.

Jessica and Kevin sat on the floor, diverting the little dog with the toys they'd bought him, while Blade stood over them, smiling at the puppy's antics. The happy mood changed when Hawkins ushered in Nina and Larry.

"Well, isn't this a charming domestic scene?" Larry asked with a mocking smile.

"It *was*," Blade answered pointedly.

"If I didn't know better, I'd say you weren't happy to see us, Cousin," Larry drawled.

"We haven't heard from you, and we wondered how you were getting along," Nina said. "It must be terribly boring for you here."

"On the contrary." Blade grinned at Jessica. "We haven't had a dull moment."

Nina and Larry exchanged a meaningful glance. "You've decided to stay, then?" she asked.

"Why would I want to leave?" Blade was beginning to enjoy himself.

Jessica moved swiftly to dispel the impression he was giving. "Blade has a very exciting new job. He's an investigative reporter for the *San Francisco Journal*."

"That's a little sad, considering the career he was forced to give up," Nina said disparagingly. "Working on a local newspaper can't be as glamorous as covering a world beat."

Jessica was annoyed, even though she knew what Nina and her brother were up to. "Blade manages to find glamour wherever he goes," she said sweetly. "He also has a new girlfriend."

Larry's eyes narrowed. "You're a fast worker."

"I wasn't speaking personally," she answered. "Blade prefers long-legged brunettes."

"Anyone in particular?" Larry asked casually.

"Jessica wasn't being accurate," Blade said with a mischievous glance at her. "I'm equally attracted to women with chestnut hair the color of autumn leaves."

"Also to blondes and redheads," she said tartly.

"Blade could never settle down with one woman," Nina remarked.

"You never know, Cousin. I might surprise you," he said.

Kevin was bored with the adult conversation. "Can I take King up to my room?" he asked Jessica.

"Yes. I'll call you when dinner is ready," she answered.

The visit wasn't going well, and Larry looked for someone to vent his anger on. "You might at least say hello before you take off," he admonished Kevin. "Didn't anybody ever teach the kid any manners?"

Jessica rushed to Kevin's defense like a ruffled mother hen. "He has excellent manners, which you might have found out if you hadn't ignored him completely until now."

Blade chuckled. "Better back off if you know what's good for you. I'm Kevin's guardian in name only. Jessica really holds the job."

"Run along, honey," she told the wide-eyed child.

"You're right. I was thoughtless," Larry apologized, not wanting to trigger an argument with her. "I'm never comfortable with kids."

"I'm sure the feeling is mutual," she answered coldly.

"Larry's never been around children." Nina stepped in to smooth things over. "He doesn't know how to talk to them."

"Like human beings." Jessica wasn't mollified.

"I'd really like to know Kevin better, but I need some coaching. Have dinner with me tonight and help me out," Larry said appealingly.

"I can't," she replied curtly. "Blade and I have dinner with Kevin every night."

"Doesn't that cut into your social life quite a bit?"

"We manage."

"I see." Larry looked at them thoughtfully, not quite sure what she was telling him. "Well, how about tomorrow? Some friends invited me to go sailing in the bay."

"By all means go. It should be a beautiful day."

"Could I have a drink, Blade?" Nina asked suddenly, to give her brother a clear field with Jessica.

"I suppose so," he answered ungraciously.

"I want to hear all about your new job. Newspaper work must be fascinating," she commented as she followed him to the bar at the far end of the room.

"A few minutes ago you considered it mundane," he answered sardonically.

"I was only sympathizing with you for having to be stuck here."

"Has anyone ever told you that you're a lot like your mother, Nina?"

"Good God, no!" She looked startled.

After his sister had coaxed Blade from the near vicinity and he could operate freely, Larry became more pressing. "Come with me tomorrow. I promise it'll be a blast. The champagne always flows like water."

"Doesn't the Coast Guard frown on sailors drinking?"

"We don't do any of the actual work. The Steffingtons have people to do that," he said dismissively.

"You had me worried for a minute," Jessica said dryly. "I thought you actually got calluses on your hands."

"You make it sound like a virtue. My friends are loaded. Why should any of us work up a sweat when they can pay somebody to do it for us?"

"I thought the fun was in sailing your own boat."

"You've been traveling with the wrong crowd. Stick with me and I'll show you what fun really is. Do we have a date?"

Jessica knew he wouldn't believe the truth—that she wouldn't consider going out with him—so she lied. "I already have a date."

"How about next weekend, then? Or one night during the week? We'll go someplace after dinner. You name the day."

"I have a lot of tentative engagements," she said lamely.

He gave her a piercing look. "Is it because of Blade? We never got along too well. Has he been poisoning your mind against me?"

"We've never discussed you." She stood up quickly, calling across the room, "I think I'll have a drink, too."

Nina looked questioningly at Larry, who shook his head slightly. She turned back to Blade saying, "I just adore this house. I remember all the holiday parties we used to have here when we were young and Aunt Adelaide was alive." That had evidently been Blade's mother.

His eyes were pensive. "She loved to have people around."

"Remember the Easter egg hunt when you and Steven dyed some raw eggs and sneaked them in with the hard-boiled ones?"

Blade smiled. "You put them in the pocket of your new dress and they broke. Larry ratted on us, and Steve and I were grounded for a week."

"We did have some good times, though. It's too bad we've grown apart."

"A lot has happened since then," Blade said bleakly.

"Time goes by so rapidly. We really should see more of each other." Nina hesitated, then said impulsively, "Why don't Larry and I stay for dinner tonight?"

Blade was caught off guard. "Well, I . . . I suppose I'd better check with Mrs. Bartlett first."

"Barty always makes enough for an army," Nina answered confidently.

Jessica wasn't any happier about the turn of events than Blade, but she realized he didn't have a choice. If Nina was sincere about wanting to bury the hatchet, though, one dinner wouldn't be such a hardship. Jessica only wished it didn't have to include Larry.

Even when he was on his good behavior, Larry was hard to take. His attempts at winning Kevin over were so patronizing that even a much younger child could have seen they were phony. Jessica continually stepped in to answer Larry's inane questions when she saw the child retreating into his shell.

The uncomfortable dinner was almost over, and Jessica was starting to breathe a sigh of relief when Nina exceeded Larry's bad taste.

She had referred back to the past again in an effort to rekindle Blade's mellow mood. He'd grown increasingly austere during dinner as he watched his nephew's reaction.

"Remember how you and Steve used to steal each other's girlfriends?" Nina asked. "You both had a new one every week."

"Scarcely. He went with Marianne his entire senior year in college." Blade glanced at Kevin's lowered head, then at Jessica. "Would you ask Mrs. Bartlett to speed up dessert?"

Nina refused to be diverted. "Maybe so, but he was crazy about Dodie Waring. He used to see her every time he came home on vacation."

"Our families were friends," Blade replied in clipped tones.

"That's probably why he didn't marry her. They pushed it too hard. Poor guy, he might be alive today if he'd married Dodie."

Kevin's face paled and his voice was almost inaudible as he asked Jessica, "May I be excused?"

"Certainly." After he left she turned on Nina with blazing eyes. "You should really be proud of yourself. You've raised insensitivity to new heights!"

"What did I do?" Nina asked. "Is mentioning my cousin's name a crime?"

"Somebody ought to put a warning label on your mouth," Jessica raged. She flung her napkin down and said to Blade, "I'll go and see if I can repair the damage she did."

She went upstairs and found Kevin lying face down on the bed. He didn't move when Jessica entered the room.

"I'm sorry about tonight," she said. He didn't answer, so she sat down next to him. "What you heard was a lot of nonsense. I can assure you that your mother and father loved each other very much."

He sat up then and looked at her, eyes bright with unshed tears. "She said they shouldn't have gotten married, that he'd still be alive if they hadn't."

"It was a foolish thing to say. As pointless as saying it would have been sunny yesterday if it hadn't rained.

What *really* happened was that your parents fell in love. They didn't want anybody but each other until you came along, and then their happiness was complete.''

''But why did she say it?'' he persisted.

''Because she's a very thoughtless woman. Some people don't consider anyone's feelings. You're bound to meet people like that in your lifetime, but fortunately there are more people like your Uncle Blade. He cares a great deal about you, as I'm sure you know by now.''

''He bought me King,'' Kevin said hesitantly.

''Because he wanted to make you happy. Did the little fellow have his dinner?'' Jessica asked, welcoming the change of subject.

''A long time ago. Can I give him a puppy biscuit?''

''Okay, but just one. You don't want to overload his tummy.''

''Can he sleep with me tonight?'' Kevin coaxed. ''It's his first night here, and he might get lonesome in a strange place.''

Jessica hesitated. Blade had said the dog should sleep in the kitchen for a week or two. The puppy was housebroken, but ''accidents'' could happen in new surroundings. Still, this was a special circumstance.

''All right, but just for tonight.''

When she left, Kevin seemed to be restored to normal. He was laughing at the puppy's clumsy attempts to chew the biscuit.

Jessica went downstairs for the sole purpose of reassuring Blade that Kevin was no longer upset. She didn't trust herself to be civil to the Kilpatrick duo. They were gone, however.

''A few more minutes and I would have assisted them out bodily,'' Blade said grimly.

"I can't believe she actually said those things in front of Kevin!"

"Her excuse was that she didn't think he'd understand."

"That says a lot for her manners as well as her common sense," Jessica remarked disgustedly.

"Enough about her. Are you sure Kevin isn't brooding? Do you think I should go up to him?"

"You can if you like, but he was playing with King when I left. I told him the puppy could sleep in his room tonight. I hope that was all right."

"It's little enough under the circumstances."

"Thank goodness for that dog," Jessica said.

"No, thank goodness for you." Blade's voice deepened. "What would we do without you?"

"I'm sure you'd manage."

"Not with any pleasure. You've turned an ordeal into an unforgettable experience."

The glow in his eyes made her chest feel oddly constricted. She laughed nervously. "That could mean either good or bad."

"I think you know what—" The telephone rang before he could finish.

The call was for Blade, and from his guarded answers, Jessica deduced that it was a woman.

"Well, yes, a little," he said, glancing cautiously at her. "Can I call you tomorrow?...No, I'm afraid I can't make it . . . Let me get back to you on that, also."

"Sorry about that. Where were we?" he asked when he returned to the couch.

"You were telling me how necessary I am to you," she answered sardonically.

"You sound as though you don't believe me."

"You can get what you require from any number of women," she said, suppressing an undercurrent of anger.

"That's not only inaccurate, it's unfair. You're implying that my only interest in a woman is getting her into bed."

"Or trying to."

"I've never made a pass at you, Jessica. Doesn't that prove something?"

"That I'm not your type, obviously."

"You must be joking! I'd like to make love to you this minute, right here on the carpet."

"You don't have to be so explicit," she said distantly.

"I'm showing restraint. If I wanted to get really graphic I'd describe how I'd unzip your dress and watch it slide off your shoulders, then slowly down to your hips. You have such a beautiful body."

"You haven't seen—" She stopped short, her cheeks flaming.

"Not the way I'd like to, gloriously nude with nothing to distract from your perfection. I want to touch you and feel you come alive."

Jessica drew in her breath sharply. "You mustn't say such things."

"I have to correct your monumental misconception that I'm indifferent to you."

"It merely confirms the fact that *any* woman turns you on," she said stubbornly.

"Not any woman. But I admit to being partial to the ones with sea green eyes and soft, smooth lips." His expression was mischievous and sensuous at the same time.

Was he telling the truth? Did Blade really find her attractive, or was he teasing her because he knew she became rattled when he turned on the charm? She looked up at him in confusion, moistening her dry lips.

"Don't do that," he groaned. "In another five seconds I'm going to kiss you, and I can't guarantee I'll stop."

Jessica had never felt so mightily torn. She couldn't deny the potent sexual attraction between them. Blade would be a marvelous lover, transporting her to magic lands on a trip unlike any other. She might even fall in love with him. But that wasn't what he wanted. It would be a purely physical experience for him, with no involvement except casual affection. That kind of relationship was unacceptable, no matter what the rewards.

"I don't know how serious you are, but it's time to back off," she said carefully. "We're in a unique situation that could easily backfire if we act irresponsibly."

"You're right, of course." He sighed. "But just for the record, I *would* like to make love to you."

"We're better off being friends."

"I hope we'll continue to be, but I have a feeling it would have been very special with you." He cupped her cheek in his palm and gazed deeply into her eyes.

Jessica felt herself melting inside when the doorbell rang.

"Who the devil is that?" Blade frowned.

A moment later Crystal came into the den. "I'm an escapee from a deadly dull party. I hoped you might rescue me, darling." The glance she gave Jessica wasn't friendly. "Or am I interrupting something?"

"Not at all," he answered. "Jessica and I had a miserable night, too."

"I know what would cheer you up," Crystal said. "Let's go dancing."

"Capital idea. I need to work off some nervous energy." His mouth curved mockingly. "Care to come along, friend?" he asked Jessica.

"No thanks. I'm not the slightest bit nervous," she answered coolly.

Jessica was amused at Crystal's relief when she refused Blade's invitation, but that was the only funny thing about the entire evening. The ease with which Blade switched his attention was downright insulting. Those passionate words that had stirred her so deeply were evidently interchangeable. They worked equally well on blondes, brunettes and redheads.

As she climbed the stairs to her room, Jessica thought about their pledge to remain friends. It was her idea, but at that moment she felt far from friendly toward Blade.

Chapter Five

Jessica and Blade weren't the only ones who had a miserable evening. After being practically thrown out of the house, Larry and Nina quarreled all the way home.

"Of all the stupid, bonehead remarks you could have made, that was the dumbest," Larry rasped.

"I don't see what was so terrible about it," Nina protested. "The way they carried on, you'd think I told the kid a dirty joke."

"It would have been better than telling him his dad was a stud."

"How did I know he'd understand? The kid is only ten years old, for God's sake!"

"You should have kept your mouth shut. What were you trying to prove with all that talk about the good old days?"

"I was trying to get Blade into a better mood. If you hadn't struck out with Jessica, we wouldn't have had to go to plan B. A fat lot of good it did us anyway. You're losing your touch, brother dear.''

"How did you expect me to score after Blade bad-mouthed me to her?" Larry scowled. "It's tough enough having to compete against his money."

"You think she's after Blade?"

"Why wouldn't she be? Our job is to see she doesn't get him."

"You made a fine start," Nina snorted.

"That was just the opening move. She'll come around."

"When donkeys fly. Face it, Larry, the Boston Strangler would have a better chance with Jessica."

"Well, maybe you're willing to fold your hands and hope for the best, but I'm not. She and Blade looked entirely too cozy tonight. We have to get her interested in someone else."

"Granted, but you're not the one. Think of somebody irresistible. Do you know any real hunks?"

He looked thoughtful for a moment. "Women go bonkers over Troy Moseby, but he has a paternity suit pending. He might be tied up in court for a while. Troy swears he isn't the father, though."

"Forget it. Who else?"

Larry pondered the question, then his eyes lit up. "Of course! Stewart Bennington. Jessica will go ape over him. He's good-looking, loaded and has a line as smooth as a baby's bottom."

Nina looked dubious. "Why would a guy like that let himself be fixed up?"

"For one thing, he owes me a favor. I covered for him in a sticky situation. But don't sell Jessica short. She's got one hell of a body and a cute little face. A guy could get lost in those big green eyes."

"If he didn't mind getting stabbed by her sharp tongue. Did you hear the way she talked to me?" Nina asked resentfully.

"We can both put up with some flak if it gets us our quarter of the estate."

"Jessica is only part of the problem. How about Blade and his mystery girlfriend? Do you have any idea who it could be?"

Larry shrugged. "Just about anybody. Blade never had trouble finding female companionship."

"As long as he keeps playing the field we don't have anything to worry about."

"We can't take anything for granted. We have to find out who she is, and if their affair is serious."

"How do you suggest we do that?" Nina asked sarcastically. "Hire a detective to follow him around?"

"That might not be a bad idea," Larry mused. "I wonder how much they cost?"

"Let's see what we can find out on our own first. I'm strapped, and you *never* have any money."

"It would be an investment, but it's too soon for drastic measures. I'll unleash Stew on Jessica, and maybe he can be our pipeline."

"What excuse will he give for calling her? If he says *you* told him to, she'll hang up on him."

"Leave it to Stewart. He's very resourceful."

"If he's like most of your friends, his definition of charm is overtipping the parking lot attendant," she answered cynically.

Jessica was out of sorts at breakfast the next morning, in contrast to Blade, who was excessively cheerful.

"You must have had a good time last night," she commented evenly.

"It was a lot of fun. You should have come along."

"Crystal had a panic attack when you suggested it."

"The invitation was sincere."

The warmth in his voice was gratifying. Jessica smiled reluctantly. "You have a lot to learn about women. If we weren't so civilized, Crystal and I would have been pulling each other's hair out."

Blade gave her a puzzled look. "I don't understand why you felt such an instant dislike for her. In the short time we've lived together I've found you to be a remarkably generous and understanding woman, yet you never gave Crystal a chance."

Jessica's good will dried up. "I'm sure she isn't losing any sleep over it."

Blade was eyeing her thoughtfully when Kevin came dashing in, followed by the puppy, whose tongue was lolling out.

"I gave King his breakfast and took him for a run on the beach," the youngster announced.

"You must have gotten up early," Jessica remarked.

"I did. King woke me up at six o'clock. He had to go outside."

"That's pretty early," Blade said.

"I didn't mind. Can he sleep in my room all the time?"

"Not until he learns to keep civilized hours."

"I got plenty of sleep. Please, Uncle Blade?"

"Possibly in a week if he settles down. Finish your breakfast and I'll give you a ride to school."

"With the top down?" the boy asked eagerly, accepting his uncle's decree without further argument.

"If that's what you want."

Jessica was pleased by their growing rapport. Kevin was talking up a storm when he and Blade went out the door together.

The house seemed very quiet after they left, although it was filled with the usual domestic noises. The daily cleaning woman was vacuuming upstairs, and a gardener was clipping hedges outside the den.

Jessica stood at the window watching him. She usually enjoyed her work, but lately she found it difficult to concentrate. It was all Blade's fault. She was entirely too involved with him. One solution would be to start dating again.

During the last weeks of Mr. Dunsmuir's illness she'd practically lived at the house. Then there had been the final arrangements and the fateful will. By now she was out of circulation, but it would only take a few phone calls to remedy the situation.

This time she could afford to be choosy, though. Henry had almost driven her crazy after Blade's practical joke, but she'd finally managed to discourage him without hurting his feelings too badly. Jessica sighed and sat down at her desk. The problem was, she didn't know anyone she did want to see.

The phone call from Larry's friend came that afternoon.

"Is this the girl with the gorgeous green eyes?" a male voice asked in throaty tones.

"What number are you calling?" Jessica asked.

"Is this Jessica Lawrence?"

"Yes. Who is this?"

"My name is Stewart Bennington. You don't know me, but a mutual friend gave me your number after I begged and pleaded and promised to make him a wealthy man."

"Who would that be?"

"Greg Mason."

"I don't know anyone by that name," she said coolly.

"Poor guy. And after he thought he'd been so charming. Did you at least enjoy the theater?"

Jessica racked her brain. Could that have been the man from Chicago who was the cousin of a college friend? Where had they gone that night? At the time she'd been dating extensively, so it was difficult to remember.

"Greg's been in and out of town like a yo-yo," Stewart said. "That's why he hasn't called lately, but he's going to. I wanted to beat him to it."

"Why?" she asked bluntly.

"After his glowing description, I knew I had to meet you."

"I'm afraid that's impossible."

"I know you're not married. Are you engaged? Involved with someone? Hopelessly in love with a paragon of all virtues?"

"Nothing that interesting. I simply don't go out on blind dates."

"Where's your spirit of adventure? We could be kindred spirits, groping our way toward each other on the freeway of life."

"That's where the major accidents occur," she said dryly. "Thanks, but no thanks."

"What can I do to persuade you? One perfect rose every day? A pass to Disneyworld?"

"I'm already living in Fantasy Land," she said a trifle grimly. "Goodbye, Mr. Bennington, I have work to do."

Jessica wondered more about who Greg Mason was than she did about Stewart Bennington, but she soon dismissed both of them from her mind.

At dinner that evening Blade mentioned that he was going to ride with the police that night while they made their rounds of Hunter's Point, an area with a high number of juvenile gangs.

"Wow! Neat!" Kevin's eyes shone. "In a real police car?"

Jessica was less enthusiastic. "That could be dangerous, Blade."

"I have to see firsthand what I'm writing about."

"Will they use the siren and that red light that spins around on top of the car?" Kevin asked.

"You never can tell." Blade smiled.

The police only used those when they were chasing someone who was often armed and dangerous, Jessica felt certain. "Couldn't you just sit in when they interrogate suspects at the police station?" she asked hesitantly.

"That's like wading in a puddle when you could be deep-sea diving," he said dismissively.

"It's a lot safer," she muttered.

He looked at her in slight surprise. "Are you worried about me?"

She managed a smile. "I've gotten used to having you around. Who would I argue with if you weren't here?"

"I'll be here, honey. You're nice to come home to." Something flickered in his eyes for a moment, then disappeared. "Don't worry, I'm indestructible."

Jessica tried to remember that when she was reading in bed after he'd gone. Blade had been through real wars and come out unscathed, but his present foray wasn't anything to take lightly. The city streets could become mine fields if gang war erupted, as the newspapers were predicting.

At one o'clock Jessica gave up the pretense of reading and tiptoed downstairs in her robe and slippers. King hadn't taken kindly to being shut in the kitchen, and she didn't want to wake him. She'd already been downstairs several times to stop him from howling.

The tranquil scene outside the den windows did nothing to calm her fears. She tensed every time a siren wailed in the distance, although common sense told her it had nothing to do with Blade. He was on the other side of town.

At two o'clock she was tempted to call the police, but Blade would never forgive her. Besides, if something *had* happened they probably wouldn't give her any information since she wasn't a relative.

When she heard a car in the driveway, Jessica rushed to the front door. Blade was barely inside the house before she launched herself into his arms, clinging so tightly that he could feel how badly she was trembling.

"What's wrong, Jessica? Has something happened to Kevin?" he asked anxiously.

"No. It's you I was worried about. You were gone so long." She buried her face in his neck, unable to stop shaking.

"Why did that worry you? I'm fine, sweetheart." He stroked her back soothingly. "Why aren't you asleep?"

"How could I sleep when I pictured you lying in a pool of blood," she said indignantly. "Where have you been all this time?"

"I told you where I was going."

"You didn't say you were going to stay out all night!"

She was so obviously overwrought that Blade didn't point out how incongruous it was for her to question his activities. He smothered a smile instead and answered meekly, "After their shift was over I took the officers out for a couple of drinks."

"You were out drinking while I was worrying myself sick?" she demanded. "That's not only inconsiderate, it's unbelievable. The bars close at two o'clock, and it's after three now.''

He couldn't help laughing. ''I had to drive all the way home from Hunter's Point. Maybe I should put a phone in the car so you can monitor my whereabouts.''

Jessica suddenly realized how badly she was overreacting. She stepped back and pulled her robe together. ''I'm glad you think it's funny. You could have gotten killed tonight.''

He reached out and smoothed her hair. ''I didn't know you cared this much.''

''Of course I care, you dimwit!'' she exclaimed in frustration. ''We're *friends*!''

''Is that what we are, Jessica?'' The blaze of excitement in his eyes was visible even in the dimly lit hall.

''That's what we . . . I mean, we can't . . .''

''We can't keep ignoring the way we feel.''

His arms closed around her, pulling her almost roughly against his taut frame. Jessica's resistance was only a reflex action. The moment their bodies met, a surge of longing swept through her. Conscious reason was overwhelmed by the need to be joined to this man, to experience the power of his body, the sensuousness of his lips. She tangled her fingers in his thick hair and pulled his head down. Uttering a low growl of satisfaction, he closed his mouth hungrily over hers.

Flames engulfed Jessica when his tongue probed deeply and his hands caressed her through the thin robe. This was what she'd fantasized about, but the realization was more earth-shattering than anything she'd imagined. As Blade parted her robe and lowered his head to trail arousing kisses over the slope of her breasts, she began to tremble.

"I've wanted you for such a long time," he murmured. "You want me, too, don't you, darling?"

"Yes, oh yes!" she whispered.

"My sweet, passionate Jessica. It's going to be so good with us."

He drew her hips against the juncture of his thighs, making her aware of his urgency. She was loosening his tie when a loud noise shattered the stillness.

The puppy had been whining for some time while they were oblivious to everything except each other. When his whimpers didn't bring results he began to howl mournfully.

The sound penetrated their consciousness, along with the housekeeper's displeased voice. A bar of light showed under the kitchen door.

"You're going to wake the whole house with your carrying on," Mrs. Bartlett scolded. "I want you to stop this nonsense and go to sleep, do you hear?"

The woman's voice was like a cold breath of reason. Jessica jerked away from Blade and wrapped her robe tightly around her trembling body. "He's been crying on and off all night," she whispered without looking at him.

"We'd better take the little mutt off her hands. King isn't Mrs. B.'s responsibility."

"You go. It wouldn't look—I don't think we should go in together."

"You're probably right." Blade's eyes were regretful as he gazed at her in the semidarkness. "Stay here. I'll send her back to bed."

Mrs. Bartlett greeted him with relief. "I don't know what we're going to do with this imp of Satan, Mr. Blade. He's been acting up something terrible. Miss Jessica's been up and down the stairs trying to quiet him, but he won't settle down."

"I'll take care of it. You get some sleep."

When the housekeeper had gone, Jessica reluctantly went into the kitchen. She dreaded having to face Blade again, but she had to take the puppy to her room. That was the only way any of them would get any sleep during what remained of the night.

Blade was down on his haunches playing with the dog, who was completely contented now that his cries had brought company. As she gazed at Blade's smiling face, Jessica had an unhappy revelation. She was in love with this man. It wasn't mere sexual attraction as she'd insisted to herself. She loved everything about him—his intelligence and sense of humor, his integrity, so many things. This was the man she wanted to spend the rest of her life with.

He scooped the dog into his arms and stood. "I understand the king has been disrupting the castle."

"We'll have to make other arrangements. I'll take him in my room tonight."

"Your rest has been disrupted enough already," Blade protested. "I'll take him."

"All right." Jessica didn't want to prolong the discussion. "Give him to me. I'll carry him upstairs, you can bring his bed."

When they made the transfer their arms brushed. Jessica flinched at the contact and ducked her head.

His eyes darkened as he noted her reaction. "I'm sorry, Jessica," he said in a muted voice.

She nodded and started toward the door, not trusting herself to answer.

What was he sorry for? she wondered later, lying sleepless in bed. That they'd been interrupted? Or that the incident had ever occurred?

Jessica groaned and turned over restlessly. How could she endure an entire year of this? She wanted him so much it was like an ache inside her. But if she settled for what he was offering, her life would become a living hell. She wanted marriage and children. He didn't even want an emotional commitment.

When the sun came up it didn't lighten the darkness of her spirits.

Kevin was eating breakfast when Jessica came downstairs the next morning, but Blade's chair was vacant. It wasn't surprising that he'd overslept after his late night. She envied him.

"Mrs. Bartlett was kind of cranky this morning," Kevin reported. "She said King kept everybody awake last night." The dog was sitting on the floor next to him.

"What's he doing down here?" Jessica asked in surprise.

"He was scratching on Uncle Blade's door, so I let him out. How did he get in there?"

"King made such a racket that your uncle had to take him to his room."

"He missed me. Can I keep him from now on?"

"I don't know. You'll have to ask your uncle," Jessica said wearily.

"Ask me what?" Blade came in, freshly shaven and looking as fit as if he'd had eight hours sleep.

"Can King stay in my room from now on?" Kevin asked.

"It's either that or we give him sleeping pills," Blade answered.

"Does that mean yes?" Kevin looked hopeful.

"A qualified one. If he keeps you awake we'll send him to a motel."

"He won't. Thanks, Uncle Blade."

When Kevin left to get his books Jessica started to follow him out of the room, but Blade stopped her.

"We have to talk about what happened last night," he said quietly.

"I've already forgotten about it," she answered quickly.

"No, you haven't, and I haven't either. But we can't let it create a wall between us. It was something that happened spontaneously. Neither of us planned it, or were responsible for it."

"It mustn't ever happen again," she said.

"Not unless you felt it was right."

"How can it be right? People with any standards don't hop into bed every time they get a biological urge. It's different when deeper feelings are involved, but we don't feel anything for each other except passion."

"That's not strictly true. We've shared a lot of experiences. We both care for Kevin." He smiled wryly. "I sound like a man trying to keep his marriage together."

His amusement at the idea caused her to lash out. "I know your views on *that* subject. You'd pass up a fortune rather than get married."

"It was supposed to be a joke," he said mildly. "But we're getting off the subject. I want to clear the air so we can go back to our old relationship."

"We never had one," she answered bitterly.

"On the contrary, we had a very rewarding one. True friendship between a man and a woman is rare, and should be cherished. I don't want my bad judgment last night to change things."

They both knew she'd been a willing participant, but Jessica couldn't bear to dwell on the fact. She still felt a rush of heat to her midsection at the memory of his hands on her body.

"All right, we're friends." She rose from her chair, anxious to get away.

His long fingers circled her wrist, preventing her from leaving. "You don't really mean that. If I promise not to touch you again, will you forgive me?"

"I suppose so." She tried to tug her hand away. "Let me go, Blade. I have work to do."

"Okay, but I'm going to convince you that I'm sincere. Let's put the whole thing behind us and go somewhere tonight."

"Go out on a date? You must be joking!"

"Not a date, just two friends who've earned a little relaxation. You hardly ever get out of the house."

"That's by choice. I turned down a date with a very persistent man just yesterday. In fact, I could hardly get rid of him." She didn't want Blade to think nobody ever asked her.

"Not Henry again?"

"No. Someone with a lot more on the ball."

"That just proves my point. You're getting into a rut. I'll get tickets for the theater tonight. What would you like to see?"

"I don't even know what's playing," she said helplessly.

"Leave it to me, then." He looked at his watch. "It's late. Got to run."

"Blade, wait! I honestly don't think this is a good idea."

"Trust me, honey. It's exactly what you need."

She went into her office with decidedly mixed feelings. The thought of spending a whole evening in Blade's company was exhilarating and frightening at the same time. She trusted him to keep his promise, but what if she betrayed her feelings in some way? Weren't they better off staying away from each other? The problem was, they couldn't maintain any meaningful distance; they were living together. Jessica sighed. The late Mr. Dunsmuir couldn't have had any idea what trouble his will would cause.

She was surprised when a huge bouquet of roses arrived for her at noon. Jessica happily assumed they were from Blade, but the card was signed, Stewart Bennington. He followed up with a phone call that afternoon.

"The flowers are beautiful, but you shouldn't have," she told him.

"I'm softening you up. Next comes candy and then perfume, followed by increasingly expensive gifts. You'll either have to go out with me, or be responsible for making me exceed my credit card limit."

"Cut up the card and save the interest charges," she advised. "I'm not going out with you."

"Meet me for a drink then. There's a little bar right near your house. I'll be the one wearing a red carnation and a happy smile—among other things, of course."

She managed to get rid of him with some difficulty. It never occurred to her to accept Stewart's invitation. Blade was the only man she wanted to be with.

Jessica was too tense to contribute much to the conversation at dinner that night, but fortunately Kevin made up for her lapse. He and his uncle found a lot to talk about. If Blade noticed her silence, he didn't comment on it.

At the end of dinner he said, "I got tickets to *Dancing In The Aisles*. I hope that's all right with you."

"How did you ever manage that?" Jessica asked. It was a Broadway musical that was reportedly sold-out.

"A good reporter always has sources. We should leave here no later than seven-thirty."

In her room, Jessica was annoyed with herself for fussing over her hair and makeup. She certainly didn't want to seem to be sending Blade any signals. But on the other hand, he would expect her to look presentable.

She looked more than that when she went downstairs a little later. Her eyes, fringed by sooty lashes, sparkled with excitement, and her face was lit by an inner glow. The white wool dress she'd chosen after much indecision was simple but effective. It displayed her curved figure admirably, and the short skirt was made for long slender legs like hers.

"Wow, you look super," Kevin exclaimed. "Doesn't she, Uncle Blade?"

"Very nice." Blade's gaze wandered over her admiringly, but his comment was restrained.

She laughed nervously. "You're both just used to seeing me look like a boy in jeans and a shirt."

"Nobody would ever mistake you for a boy," Blade said.

The musical relaxed Jessica. By intermission she was really enjoying herself.

"I think you're right," she remarked as they stood in the lobby. "I should get out more. It gives one a whole new perspective."

"I'm surprised a woman as beautiful as you doesn't have men lining up outside the door."

"You have to include a lot of Henrys if you go in for quantity. I prefer quality."

"You haven't found anyone who meets your requirements?" he asked casually.

"Not yet, but I keep hoping," she answered brightly.

"What are you looking for in a man?"

"The same qualities you mentioned—intelligence and a sense of humor to start with." She laughed slightly. "I'm more apt to be successful in my search than you are. I don't have to worry about anyone marrying me for my money."

"Fifty thousand dollars is a sizable chunk."

"That's small change to you."

"Would you like to be rich, Jessica?" He watched her with an unreadable expression.

"Who wouldn't? I love having someone else clean the house and cook for me. Luxury is addictive." She smiled. "To answer your question, yes, I'd like to be rich."

The warning buzzer sounded and Blade said, "We'd better return to our seats."

When the musical was over Jessica was enthusiastic. "It was worth all the raves. Thanks for a lovely evening, Blade."

"I'm glad you enjoyed it." As they walked past the Langley Hotel he said, "I'm hungry. How about you?"

"I could eat," she admitted, not having had much dinner.

"Let's go to Rubies." It was a trendy disco on the top floor of the hotel.

The decor could have been described as turn-of-the-century bordello. Everything was done in a deep ruby red, including the walls and carpeting. Even the lights cast a rosy glow. The place was very crowded, but Blade got a table.

"The pasta is good if that appeals to you," he remarked as they looked at menus.

"You've been here before?" she asked. Rubies had been open only a few months.

He nodded. "Once."

This might be where he and Crystal went the night she wanted to go dancing. But Jessica was determined not to let that bother her. Why allow the other woman to spoil a nice evening? It was a needed reminder, however, that Blade was only on loan.

After they'd given their order he asked her to dance. As soon as she moved into his arms, Jessica knew it hadn't been a good idea. Her body conformed to his with the ease of familiarity. She knew the feeling of his broad shoulders under her arm, the sensuous brush of his thighs against hers. The clean male scent of his skin filled her nostrils like an aphrodisiac.

She wanted to pull away but that would have been too pointed. Jessica suffered silently as they circled the floor, joined together in a symbolic way that brought only frustration. It was a relief when the music changed to a rapid beat and they were buffeted by more energetic dancers. That gave her a valid reason for suggesting they return to their table. Blade agreed swiftly, as though he, too, knew it had been a mistake.

The arrival of their food provided the needed distraction. By the time the waiter finished sprinkling grated cheese over the pasta and poured the wine, the constraint they'd felt had disappeared.

Blade displayed all the charm he was famous for. He told Jessica funny stories about his boyhood in San Francisco, and the more humorous aspects of his present job.

"You never talk about your work in the Near East," she commented finally. "Don't you miss it?"

"Like an aching tooth," he said, suddenly grim faced.

Hope thrilled through her. "Does that mean you won't be going back when the year is up?"

"I have to go back," he said quietly.

Jessica's hope plummeted like a bird with a broken wing. "That doesn't make much sense if you don't want to."

"I have to keep a commitment I made."

Was Blade involved with a woman over there? But why wouldn't he bring her here for this year? In fact, why didn't he marry her if he felt such a strong attachment? A lot of money hinged on his marrying. Perhaps Mr. Dunsmuir hadn't approved, and Blade didn't want to profit by going against his father's wishes.

"You're very quiet all of a sudden," he remarked.

"I'm just surprised," she faltered. "Now that you're getting along so well with Kevin and you have such an interesting job, I thought you were fairly happy here. I didn't realize you were counting the days."

"I'm not. I'll have to go back for a while when the year is up, but I'll return to San Francisco eventually."

"It will be hard on Kevin when you leave."

"I'll keep in close touch with him, and I'll try to come home on holidays."

"It won't be the same. I hope he doesn't regress," she said with a worried frown.

"He won't. I'll explain it to him. But why are we worrying about that now? I'm not leaving for a long time."

The waiter brought coffee, and the subject was dropped. It had cast a pall over the evening, however.

Their former light mood was restored on the drive home when they passed the theater that was showing *Bread and Hollyhocks*.

"I never did get to see that film," Blade remarked.

"You didn't miss anything."

"Would it have been better if you'd seen it with some-one other than Henry?"

"It would have been rotten even if I'd been sitting on Tom Selleck's lap."

Blade grinned. "That's pretty bad. How about taking a chance on a spaghetti western tomorrow night?"

"If you don't mind, I'd rather see a movie without subtitles."

"Okay, what about the new film at the Crown? It's a murder mystery with a twist. The victim actually dies of natural causes."

"How can it be murder then?"

"That's the twist."

When they went into the house Jessica's constraint re-turned. She was used to saying good-night at the door after a casual date. There was a feeling of intimacy about walking up the stairs together.

"Well...uh...good-night," she said when they reached her bedroom.

"Good-night, honey. See you in the morning," he an-swered without any of her discomfort.

The next few days were all that Jessica could have wished for. She and Blade went to the movies and the ballet. Another night they barbecued hot dogs on a grill he carried down to the beach. Afterward they cast fish-ing lines from the water's edge until it got dark. Then when Kevin had gone to bed, they watched television in the den.

Jessica curled up on the couch and Blade sat on the floor with his long legs stretched out and his head rest-ing against the edge of the sofa. They were a deceptive picture of domesticity, Jessica thought wryly, but she was filled with a deep contentment.

When she couldn't resist smoothing his thick dark hair, he glanced around and smiled at her. "I was brushing away some sand," she said quickly.

Stewart continued to call every day, but Jessica had even less interest in meeting him. She was beginning to hope she really meant something to Blade. Why else would he spend all his free time with her? He continued to get phone calls, but he didn't accept or make any dates.

Jessica's bubble burst when Blade called the next afternoon to tell her he wouldn't be home for dinner that night.

"But I thought... What about Kevin?" she asked. "He expects us to be here with him."

"We have been for weeks. He doesn't need us anymore. It's time we all started living normal lives."

"I wasn't aware that we weren't," she answered stiffly.

"People do occasionally have dinner out."

"By all means go, then. You don't have to report to me."

"I thought I should let Mrs. Bartlett know. Will you tell her for me?"

"Certainly."

Her clipped tone made Blade hesitate. "Did you have something you wanted to do tonight?"

"Nothing I can't do alone."

"I'm sorry to spring this on you at such short notice, but Crystal left a message for me at the paper about a political dinner she has tickets to."

"I didn't know Crystal was interested in politics."

"She probably isn't, but she knows I am. I'm doing a series on influence peddling and its possible ties to organized crime."

"You're going to delve into the subject tonight? That should be a lot of chuckles for Crystal."

"I don't have time to discuss her intellectual capacity with you," he said impatiently. "I'll see you tomorrow."

Jessica slammed down the receiver angrily. The nerve of the man! After she'd given up every evening to have dinner with *his* nephew, *he* decides he can't be bothered any longer. Without even discussing it with her! It served her right for being such a patsy. Blade probably expected her to take over his responsibility while he was free to enjoy himself. Well, he was due for a surprise. She'd wasted enough time on the Dunsmuir family.

Jessica paced the floor furiously, unwilling to admit the truth. Blade had never asked her to restrict her activities, and Kevin no longer needed their constant company. He had even requested permission to stay over at a friend's house on the coming weekend.

That wasn't the point, though, Jessica insisted to herself. Blade had gone out of his way to make her think they were a devoted family, and sap that she was, she'd fallen for it. But no more! He could save all his charm for Crystal and her ilk. Jessica Lawrence was immune.

Chapter Six

The silver BMW pulled up to the front door of the Dunsmuir house and parked, but the three people inside didn't get out. They continued the animated conversation they were having.

"I don't know how I let you talk me into this," Stewart Bennington said.

"Larry's full of good ideas that never work," Nina answered mockingly.

Other than giving her a poisonous look, Larry ignored his sister. "Your reputation is at stake," he told his friend.

"You win some, you lose some." Stewart shrugged. "I gave it my best shot, but that woman could freeze ice cubes."

"You can thaw her out," Larry insisted. "We should have tried the direct approach in the first place. It's too easy to fluff somebody off over the phone."

"You expect her to fall for the story you dreamed up?"

"Piece of cake." After a moment Larry hedged his bet. "The worst that can happen is you'll get a tan."

"You think I gave up my day to lie on a public beach with you when I could be playing tennis at the club? Or at least be having a decent lunch."

"Jessica will weaken," Larry soothed.

"We'd better go inside and get it over with," Nina remarked. "The sooner we're in, the sooner we'll be out."

"If you're so sure we're going to fall flat on our faces, why did you come along?" Larry asked furiously.

Nina grinned. "Somebody has to drive home after Jessica cuts you both off at the knees—and it's more fun than selling dresses."

Hawkins answered the door and showed them to the den where Jessica was typing furiously.

Her frown deepened to a scowl when she looked up and saw the visitors. "Just what I needed," she muttered under her breath.

"You're certainly earning your keep," Larry observed with a condescending smile that set her teeth on edge.

"Blade is at work," she said curtly, wanting to add, why aren't you?

"We didn't come to see him, we came to use the beach."

She shrugged. "Go ahead. It's open to the public. You could have used the path in the cul-de-sac."

"I wanted to leave my purse here," Nina said after a prompting look from Larry. "I guess the fellows should leave their valuables, too, in case we decide to go swimming. I don't suppose anyone will take our clothes," she added with a dubious expression.

"You can leave your clothes in one of the guest rooms if you like," Jessica said indifferently.

"That's a very provocative invitation." Stewart spoke up for the first time.

"What's the matter with me?" Larry exclaimed. "I haven't introduced you two. This is my friend, Stewart Bennington."

"We've met, in a way," Stewart said.

"You know each other?" Larry asked in mock astonishment.

"Not as well as I'd like to." Stewart regarded her with unfeigned admiration. "All the reports were correct. You are enchanting."

Jessica was outraged as she got the picture. No wonder she couldn't remember Greg Mason. He didn't exist. Larry had given Stewart her number and egged him on. But why? Did he honestly think she was after Blade for his money? The idea was laughable under the circumstances, also insulting.

"I've been thinking a lot about you," she said to Stewart. When his eyes lit up she added, "Tell me more about Greg Mason. I can't for the life of me place him."

"Why would I remind you of another man when I want you to concentrate on me?" he asked smoothly.

"Because I asked you to," she answered evenly.

"Come to the beach with us," Larry put in hastily. "You can talk about it there."

"Unlike the rest of you, I'm a working woman," she said.

"Blade's fortunate to have such a devoted employee," Nina drawled.

She had unwittingly hit a sore spot. That was exactly what Jessica was. Not a member of the family, not a friend, merely an unappreciated employee. Why shouldn't she take an hour off if she felt like it? What difference did it make if Nina and Larry were trying to fix her up with Stewart out of paranoia? He was presentable at least.

She took a good look at him for the first time, and wasn't displeased by what she saw. Stewart Bennington was conventionally handsome. His blond hair was expensively cut, and his casual clothes were of impeccable quality. He was also tall and athletically built. Not as tall or as trim as Blade, but why compare the two? Jessica was annoyed with herself at the fleeting thought.

"Please come with us," Stewart was urging.

"Well, maybe for an hour. I could use some fresh air."

When Stewart suggested the two of them take a walk along the beach, Jessica accepted. Let Larry and Nina think their plan was working. At least she wouldn't have to spend any time with them.

"Are you and Larry good friends?" she asked as they strolled along the sand.

"I guess you could say so. We were in school together, and he sold me my condominium."

Jessica's lip curled. "Unlike Blanche DuBois, he's never been dependent on the charity of strangers."

"Larry can get on your nerves a bit, but he's not such a bad guy."

"Compared to a typhoid carrier?"

"He told me his cousin had done a number on him with you."

"Larry can turn people off on his own," she answered coldly. "Blade has nothing to do with it."

"Blade was in school with us, too, but we weren't close friends. How does he like being back in San Francisco?"

"All right, I guess," she answered neutrally.

"He seemed to be enjoying himself when I saw him the other night. The girl he was with looked familiar, but I couldn't remember her name," Stewart remarked casually.

"Crystal Hansen, no doubt."

"Oh, sure, now I remember."

"I'd better be getting back," Jessica said abruptly.

"Not yet," he protested. "I haven't had a chance to find out anything about you."

"Why don't you ask Greg Mason?"

"Okay, I'm a fraud, but it was in good cause." He smiled disarmingly. "I really did want to meet you."

"Why?"

"Because Larry told me you had a drop-dead figure and a cute little face. But he was wrong." After a pause, Stewart deepened his voice. "You have an exquisite face."

"The baloney I get at the market usually comes sliced," she commented dryly.

"Surely you know how lovely you are. I'm not the first man who's told you."

"No, you all tend to use overkill."

"Don't you like compliments?"

"When they're sincere."

"All right, how's this? Your nose is too short, but I happen to like short noses."

She laughed. "Now you're getting the hang of it."

"I've never been honest with a woman before. It's a little frightening."

"Everything is the first time, but hang in there. You might become proficient."

"I also might never get another date. You'll have to go out with me to keep up my morale."

"You're being tricky again."

"You can't expect an instant miracle. Will you go out with me tonight, Jessica?"

She hesitated for only a moment. Stewart wasn't her dream date, but he was mildly amusing, and his obvious interest was just what she needed right now. Of course there was always the chance that he was only acting on Larry's instructions, but Jessica was experienced enough about men to doubt that was his only motivation. It didn't matter anyway. She wanted to start dating again, and Stewart was available.

"I'd be happy to go out with you tonight," she said.

"Wonderful. What time shall I pick you up? Larry said you don't accept dinner invitations."

"Larry has yet to get anything right about me. I'd love to go to dinner," she said firmly.

After she'd gone back to the house, Larry questioned Stewart eagerly. "Did everything go okay? Did you get a date with her?"

"Naturally. Did you doubt it?" Stewart said smugly.

"What do you have to say now, Miss Negative Nellie?" Larry crowed to Nina. "Am I a genius, or what?"

"I think I deserve some of the credit, old man," Stewart commented. "I also found out that bit of information you wanted. Blade's girlfriend is Crystal Hansen."

"The tall, leggy brunette? Isn't she the one Toddy Newhouse was so crazy about?"

Stewart looked at him significantly. "If I were you, I'd start worrying."

"Maybe I unleashed you on the wrong girl."

"Forget it," Stewart advised. "Jessica is a living doll."

"You owe me one," Larry said tentatively.

"I just paid off with interest." Stewart gave him a satisfied smile. "But if things go the way I expect, I'll owe you another one."

* * *

Jessica had a surprisingly good time that night, partly because she was determined to. They started the evening at the Grotto, a restaurant owned by a famous chef from Los Angeles. The eating place had a long waiting list for reservations, but Stewart had no trouble getting in at short notice. He and Jessica were shown to a table immediately.

"I'm impressed," she said as they bypassed the crowd of waiting patrons.

"I hoped you would be."

"You don't happen to be a restaurant critic? I understand they get the best tables."

He shook his head. "That would entail going to all those dreary little ethnic places where it's best not to ask what you're eating."

"You're a terrible snob. Other cultures simply use different kinds of food. That doesn't make them bad."

"I don't want to change their eating habits. I simply have an aversion to consuming anything that civilized people either stomp on, or keep as pets."

"How gross!" Jessica made a face.

He grinned. "You asked, and I told you. That's the downside of being truthful."

The waiter arrived with menus, and for a while they concentrated on choosing from the large selection of dishes offered. Stewart made several recommendations and described how they were prepared. Then he conferred at length with the wine steward on the proper wine to accompany their meal. Stewart seemed as knowledgeable about vintages and years as the other man.

After they were alone once more Jessica said, "If you aren't a restaurant critic, you must have something to do with food. What do you do?"

"As little as possible. My grandfather left me a rather sizable trust fund."

"You mean, you don't do *anything*?" she asked incredulously.

"I do a great deal. I play tennis and handball. I go sailing, and I have a ski lodge in Tahoe and a condo in Palm Springs. Those things more than fill up my days."

"If you've never held a job, what are you going to say you're retired from when you get older?"

"I'm never going to get old," he said confidently. "Certainly not in spirit."

Jessica felt sorry for him. Stewart would grow old, frittering away his time, still thinking he was captivating to young women who would laugh at him behind his back. Blade, on the other hand was just as rich, yet he lived life on the cutting edge and would make an even greater name for himself in his senior years. How could two men from the same background be so different?

"You look disapproving," Stewart commented. "I suppose you're comparing me to Blade."

Jessica was startled at his discernment. "Why would I do that?" she hedged.

"Larry says you find Blade quite attractive."

"And you're the red herring that's supposed to distract me," she said mockingly.

"That was the plan," Stewart admitted.

"Why are you telling me?"

"Because you already knew it anyway. One thing puzzles me, though. Why did you agree to go out with me under the circumstances?"

"Perhaps I found you more charming in person," she said lightly.

"I'd like to think so, but you aren't sending out those signals." He gazed at her consideringly. "Is Larry right? Does Blade have the inside track?"

"Don't be ridiculous! Larry told you everything else, so I'm sure he told you the terms of Mr. Dunsmuir's will. Blade and I are simply trying to make the best of an unfortunate situation."

"I'll bet Blade doesn't think it's so bad."

"We have very little to do with each other. He has his friends, and I have mine."

After staring at her intently for a moment Stewart said, "Against all odds, I'm inclined to believe you." He gave a slight laugh. "If Blade is tied up with Crystal Hansen, he has his hands full."

"I really don't care to discuss his personal life," Jessica said distantly.

"Neither do I, now that I know you're not part of it," he answered deeply.

"You're wasting your seduction on the wrong woman," she told him crisply. "Larry will undoubtedly assign you to Crystal next."

"You don't have a very high opinion of me, do you?" She shrugged. "It doesn't matter what I think."

"It does to me—surprisingly. I know that sounds like I'm blowing smoke at you, but I find you a very exciting woman. I've never met anyone quite like you."

"That's because you seldom encounter the working classes," she remarked dryly.

"Is it my money you object to? That makes you a bit of a snob, too, doesn't it?"

"I have nothing against money," she said slowly. "It's your life-style I don't understand. I can't imagine spending all my time simply enjoying myself."

"Have you ever tried it?"

"No," she admitted.

"I'd like to contribute to your education if you'll let me."

"I'm a working woman," she reminded him.

"Not twenty four hours a day. Have you ever gone sailing in a hot air balloon?"

"No."

"We'll do that on Sunday, after the dance at the country club Saturday night. It's a costume party. I'm not wild about dressing up as a pirate or a court jester, so how would you feel about going as Fred Astaire and Ginger Rogers?"

"We'd simply be wearing evening clothes."

"I was afraid you'd figure that out. All right, you get to choose the costumes, as long as they aren't clown suits. Under no circumstances will I wear baggy pants."

"I can't imagine you in them." She laughed. "Even your bathing trunks had a crease, I noticed."

"Doesn't everyone's?"

Stewart took it for granted that she'd accepted his invitations, and Jessica saw no reason not to. The way he spent his life was his business. A constant pursuit of pleasure wouldn't be to her taste, but she didn't object to small doses.

After dinner they went dancing. Stewart first suggested Rubies, but Jessica vetoed that idea. She had no interest in a chance meeting with Blade and Crystal, although having him see that she also had a date was tempting. Not tempting enough, however.

Instead, Stewart took her to a series of nightclubs south of Market Street. The area was currently one of the "in" places to go. During the day it was industrial, but after business hours, a series of funky clubs and discos opened like night-blooming flowers.

Stewart knew them all. He led her from one to another until Jessica finally called a halt.

"If we hit every spot tonight, you won't have anything to do the rest of the week," she protested.

"That's never happened yet. Come on, we haven't been to Ruffles yet."

"It's almost two o'clock, they'll be closing."

"We can look in for a few minutes, and then I know of an after-hours place."

Jessica didn't get home until almost three-thirty. If anyone had asked her, she would have said that kind of evening would get boring, but the sheer novelty of it kept her amused.

"Tomorrow night we'll take up where we left off," Stewart said when she finally insisted on going home.

She turned him down. "Tomorrow night I plan to flake out early. You'll probably sleep until noon, but I have to get up and go to work in the morning."

"Nobody's going to fire you if you take the day off," he said dismissively.

"I won't bother to argue with you because I know you wouldn't understand."

"Is this where I get another lecture on being responsible?"

"No, you're a hopeless case." She smiled to take away the sting.

"You did have a good time, though, didn't you?"

"I had a super time."

"You sound surprised." He laughed. "I'll make a convert of you yet."

"My first lesson went into overtime. It's scandalously late, Stewart. I have to go in."

When they reached the front door, he framed her face in his palms. "All joking aside, I had a perfectly smashing time tonight."

His lips met hers in a kiss that wasn't chaste, yet it wasn't anything to object to, either. Jessica didn't pull away. She waited to feel something. Stewart was a handsome man; he would fulfill the dreams of many women. He had a lot of qualities to recommend him, including expertise in the romance department. His kiss was a masterpiece of subtlety.

Unfortunately, Blade's image kept intruding. It was his mouth she wanted to feel moving over hers, his arms she wanted to walk into.

Stifling a sigh she stepped back. "Thanks for a lovely evening, Stewart."

"Until Saturday, then," he said reluctantly.

Jessica tiptoed up the stairs, but her caution was unnecessary. Blade came charging out of his room as she was trying to avoid the squeaky board in the hall.

"Where the hell have you been?" he demanded.

"I was out," she answered, startled at seeing him. "What are you doing up at this hour?" It was almost a replay of the night she waited up for *him*.

"I was worried about you, damn it! Where were you?"

"You're not the only one who's allowed to have a date."

"You had a date? Who with?"

Her temper rose at his ill-concealed surprise. "That doesn't happen to be any of your business."

His eyes were the color of steel. "I have a right to know as long as you're living in my house."

"Not by choice," she flared.

"That's beside the point."

The puppy started to whine, disturbed by their voices. "Now see what you've done!" Jessica scolded. "Next you'll wake Kevin."

"I'll wake up the whole damn house if I don't get some answers." Taking her arm in a firm grip, Blade pushed her into her bedroom and closed the door behind them. "All right, start talking."

"This is outrageous!" she stormed. "You have no right to question me."

"As I recall, you gave *me* the third degree."

"That was different. You were out dodging bullets. I was on a date."

"Which brings us back to where we started. Who were you with, and where were you this late? As you informed me, every place closes at two."

"Stewart knew of an after-hours spot."

"Stewart who?"

"Stewart Bennington, if you must know."

Jessica was annoyed at herself for letting him worm the information out of her. Not that it mattered. But Blade had no right to be so masterful when he had been out with Crystal. He was probably just annoyed that she'd shown him up by staying out later.

He was frowning. "Is that Larry's friend? The one who spends all his time working on his tan and chasing women?"

"Stewart happens to be a very charming man," she answered angrily.

"He's a parasite who never worked a day in his life."

"He doesn't have to work. He's rich."

"I could give you some notable examples of wealthy men who contributed to society. Some of them were presidents of this country."

"Everyone can't be president, the ballot would be too long." She took refuge in flippancy, unwilling to admit Blade was right.

His eyes narrowed. "You admire Bennington's life-style?"

"Why not? I don't find a rich man less appealing than a poor one."

"It might even add to his allure?" Blade asked sarcastically.

"It's possible," she agreed, not prepared to back down.

His mouth curled in disgust. "You really picked yourself a winner."

"Now that you've given me your seal of approval, will you kindly get out of my room?"

"Gladly!" He strode out, slamming the door.

Jessica held her breath, but King didn't make any outcry. She was thankful for small favors, but Blade had made her too angry to sleep. The unmitigated gall of the man! He was furious because she hadn't been keeping the home fires burning while he was out with his sexy girlfriend. Well, he'd better get used to it. She was through being old faithful!

Jessica wished they could break the breakfast ritual as easily as they could arrange to be out for dinner, but it would make more work for Mrs. Bartlett. Jessica would have gladly gotten her own breakfast, but she knew the housekeeper wouldn't let her.

The scant amount of sleep she'd had didn't improve Jessica's mood. She went downstairs the next morning feeling grim, and the fact that Kevin was late as usual made matters worse. She and Blade were always careful to be civil to each other in front of the child.

Blade's expression wasn't encouraging, but his greeting was courteous. After they'd said good morning, however, neither could think of anything else to say. Mrs. Bartlett broke the impasse by coming in to ask what Jessica wanted for breakfast.

"Just toast and coffee," she said.

"That's not enough to eat," the older woman scolded.

Jessica mustered a smile. "I'm only eating *that* to please you. I'm really not hungry."

"You look kind of peaked. I hope you're not coming down with something."

"I'm fine. I didn't have much sleep last night, that's all." Jessica regretted the admission as soon as it was out. Why had she opened the door for another argument?

But Blade surprised her. "I suppose I should apologize for last night," he said when the housekeeper had left the room.

"Why don't we just forget it?"

"Bad feelings don't go away if you simply ignore them. You're angry at me because I lost my temper, and I'm annoyed with you because you did a thoughtless thing."

"How did you twist things around to that conclusion?" she asked angrily. "You were the one who made a date first!"

He stared at her intently. "Is that why you went out with Bennington?"

"Certainly not. And I don't want to listen to any more character assassination."

"Don't worry, I've had my say on the subject. When I said you were thoughtless, I meant for disappearing without telling anyone you were leaving."

"Mrs. Bartlett knew, since I wasn't here for dinner."

"That's all she knew, not where you went or with whom. As you stated in no uncertain terms at the outset, this is not a hotel. We don't come and go anonymously. If I overreacted last night I'm sorry, but there *is* a precedent for it.'' A faint smile dispelled some of his sternness for a moment. ''Since you hadn't mentioned any plans, I couldn't imagine where you'd gone. I was extremely worried when it got so late.''

A glow warmed the chill around Jessica's heart. Blade was worried about her! It was a small thing, yet gratifying. ''I'm sorry,'' she murmured. ''It was a spur of the moment decision.''

''I didn't even know you knew Bennington.''

''I didn't until yesterday. Larry and Nina brought him over. They were going to the beach, and they wanted to leave their clothes here.''

Blade raised one eyebrow. ''Was the Yacht Club quarantined?''

His failure to guess the real reason the Kilpatricks introduced her to Stewart was discouraging. It meant he couldn't conceive of anyone thinking he might fall in love with her.

''Who knows why your cousins do anything?'' she asked dismissively. ''I'm simply telling you what happened. Stewart and I sort of hit it off, and he asked me out.''

''I see.'' Blade's austerity deepened. ''Well, in the future I'd appreciate it if you'd leave me a note.''

''Maybe I should carry a beeper so you'll know where I am at all times.''

''I'm sorry if you feel pressured,'' he answered coldly.

''It was only a joke,'' she said hastily. ''You said something like that to me the night I took you apart for being late.'' Her cheeks turned rosy as they gazed at each other, remembering how that night had ended. She averted her eyes. "You're perfectly right. I should have left a note. I will in the future."

"You must have enjoyed yourself."

"I'm sure you did, too. How was your dinner with Crystal?"

"Most interesting."

"That's nice."

Their conversation was grinding to a halt when Kevin arrived and provided a diversion.

Jessica and Blade were scrupulously polite to each other for the next couple of days. Both made a point of informing the other of future plans. It was an uneasy truce, however. They were so busy watching every word that they couldn't think of anything to say. Without Kevin, dinnertime would have been torture. He was always bubbling over with things to talk about. But one night he was uncharacteristically quiet.

"Is something bothering you, Kevin?" Jessica looked at his bowed head with a slight frown.

"No," he murmured.

"Is everything all right at school?" Blade asked with the same concern.

"Yes."

"We can tell something's wrong. Wouldn't you feel better if you told us about it," Jessica asked gently.

"Tonight is parents' night at school," he mumbled.

Jessica and Blade exchanged a look of compassionate understanding. "Would you like us to go with you?" she asked.

"You're not my parents," he said hesitantly. "I don't know if you can."

"I'm your guardian," Blade said. "That's the next best thing. And Jessica is, well, she's your best friend."

"Do you think it will be all right?" Dawning hope filled the youngster's face.

"We'll be the classiest family there," Blade assured him.

Kevin was very quiet in the car, not responding when Jessica and Blade tried to draw him out. It was uncomfortably reminiscent of their early days together, although the youngster wasn't being sullen. Jessica's heart ached for him, knowing what he was going through. Nothing made a child feel more insecure than being different from his peers.

When they reached the school some of his friends were running up and down the hallway while their harried parents tried to corral them. Several of the boys urged Kevin to join them, but he didn't leave Jessica and Blade's side.

They waited their turn to talk to the teacher, a pleasant-faced older woman who was surrounded by mothers, fathers and their offspring.

When the crowd around her thinned out the teacher turned to them with a warm smile. "I'm Mrs. Cassidy. Hello, Kevin. These must be your parents."

"I'm Blade Dunsmuir, Kevin's uncle," Blade spoke up quickly. "And this is Jessica."

"Oh, of course." A shade of discomfort crossed the woman's face as she remembered Kevin's status. "I'm so glad you could come."

"We're very interested in anything that concerns Kevin," Blade said. "How is he doing in class?"

"Kevin is one of my best students. You can be very proud of him."

"That's certainly good to hear." Blade smiled.

Jessica knew their time with the teacher would be necessarily brief. She wanted to use it to find out more pressing things than Kevin's scholastic achievement, but not in front of him.

Mrs. Cassidy intercepted her troubled glances at the boy, and interpreted them correctly. "Why don't you go out in the hall with your friends while we finish talking," she suggested to Kevin. "We won't be long." When he'd gone she said to Jessica, "Did you want to ask me something?"

"I was wondering how Kevin gets along with the other children."

"He was a bit difficult at first," the woman admitted.

"He had been through a great deal," Jessica told her earnestly. "Is there anything we should be doing to help?"

"Kevin has adjusted very nicely," Mrs. Cassidy soothed. "You have nothing to worry about. He's a fine young man, Mrs. Dunsmuir."

Blade took Jessica's hand and smiled at the teacher. "Thank you, Mrs. Cassidy. We think so."

As they left the room, Jessica asked, "Do you suppose I should have told her?"

"Why confuse matters further?"

"I guess you're right, but it made me uncomfortable."

He let go of her hand. "I'm sorry you feel that way."

"It has nothing to do with you," she said impatiently. "I only meant she might think I was being presumptuous if she knew I'm not even distantly related to Kevin."

"You care more about him than people who are," he said huskily.

"Who could help it? He's a fine young man." She smiled as she repeated the teacher's words.

Good relations had been restored between Jessica and Blade by the time they caught up with Kevin. He was back to normal now that the ordeal was over and no one had made a big deal out of the fact that he was an orphan. Kevin and another boy were talking animatedly beside a man and woman.

When they walked over to him he said, "Gary's parents are taking him for ice cream. Can we go, too?"

"Sure, if Gary's parents don't mind having company," Blade said.

"We'd be delighted," the woman answered.

"Gee, great!" The two boys punched each other happily, then ran down the hall to the exit.

"I'm Ruth Crenshaw," Gary's mother said, "and this is my husband, Harry."

"Nice to meet you. I'm Blade Dunsmuir, and this is Jessica." This time Blade omitted mentioning that he was Kevin's uncle.

Jessica looked up at him with a slight frown. Did he realize what he'd done? She wanted to set the record straight about both of them. Then they'd think she was Blade's girlfriend.

He made matters worse by putting his arm around her shoulders and saying, "The boys are waiting. Let's go, honey."

"Good idea," Harry agreed. "The sooner we get there, the sooner we can go home."

"He's having a fit about missing the baseball game on TV." Ruth heaved an exasperated sigh. "Husbands are impossible at times, aren't they?" she remarked to Jessica.

"They certainly are." Jessica put her arm around Blade's waist and pinched him sharply.

"Ouch!" he yelped.

"Is something wrong?" she asked sweetly.

"Nothing I can think of, my love." He grinned and planted a kiss on top of her head.

After the boys had eaten their hot-fudge sundaes, they pleaded to be allowed to play the video games that lined one wall of the big room. Blade supplied the quarters, and they rushed off, leaving the adults to finish their ice cream.

While the men talked sports Ruth remarked to Jessica, "You look so young to have a ten-year-old child. You must have gotten married in your teens."

"Well, actually... Blade and I aren't married." Color swiftly stained Jessica's cheeks. "I mean, I'm not Kevin's mother."

"Oh, I didn't realize. You seem to have such a close relationship."

"I'm very fond of Kevin," Jessica said.

"He's a lucky boy. So often stepmothers resent having to take care of someone else's child. I can tell that won't be a problem for you."

"I'm afraid you've gotten the wrong idea about us. Blade and I are just good friends."

"Whatever you say." Ruth obviously didn't believe her.

And who could blame her? Jessica thought. Blade's sense of humor was really annoying at times. His behavior tonight would give anyone the impression that they were in love. Jessica had a sudden, chilling thought. Maybe he wasn't solely to blame. She always reacted to Blade's slightest touch. Right now his hand on her shoulder seemed to be burning through her blouse to the skin underneath. Was that apparent to a casual onlooker? More importantly, did Blade have a clue?

"We'd better get the boys home," she said abruptly. "Tomorrow is a school day."

Chapter Seven

Jessica waited to reprimand Blade until after Kevin had gone to bed and they were alone in the den.

"I suppose you realize your behavior tonight was outrageous," she chided.

"I thought I was a model father." He chuckled. "Of course you deserve some of the credit. Having such an adorable mother for my child helped."

"That's not funny. After the performance you put on, Ruth took it for granted that we were engaged or something."

"The 'or something' sounds interesting?" he teased.

"But not the engaged part?" she asked coldly.

Blade's eyes were enigmatic but he continued to smile. "Are you trying to marry me for love or money?"

"Don't flatter yourself!" she flared. "I'm not in the market for a husband. But if I were, you wouldn't be on my shopping list."

"You might put a sense of humor on the list," he commented mildly. "You seem to have lost yours."

Jessica's lashes fluttered down. She was doing it again, telegraphing her emotions. "I'm sorry," she murmured. "I was afraid you were making problems for Kevin."

"If you'd let Ruth assume we were married, she would have lost interest in the subject."

"That could lead to complications," Jessica said stubbornly.

"All right, next time we go to one of these things I'll say, 'This is Jessica. We're neither engaged nor married. We live together, but it's strictly platonic.'"

"You don't have to go that far," she said stiffly.

"Will you please tell me what you do want?" he asked patiently.

"I don't know, but it's over with anyway. With any luck they won't have another of these functions this year."

Blade walked to the window and stared out with his hands bunched in his pockets. They were both thinking about next year when none of them would be together like this.

"It's beautiful out," he remarked finally. "Care to take a walk along the beach?"

"Good idea. I'm stuffed from that hot-fudge sundae."

A full moon lit up the beach and silvered a sequin path over the dark ocean. In contrast, the lights illuminating the Golden Gate Bridge were loops of golden beads suspended in the air.

They walked silently along the sand for a while, keeping a careful distance apart, until Jessica got a pebble in her shoe.

"Ow! Wait a minute," she said.

When she tried to stand on one foot to take off her shoe, Blade put his arm around her waist. "Here, lean on me."

"That really hurt." She dumped out the small rock.

"Why don't you take off your shoes? You'll only get more sand in them." Blade had removed his own shoes and left them at the bottom of the steps.

"I'd have to take off my stockings, too," she objected.

"So?"

Jessica had on panty hose. If she took them off she wouldn't have anything on under her dress. But it was either that or continue to be uncomfortable.

"Okay, turn around," she ordered.

He seemed amused, but he complied. His amusement deepened when Jessica discovered she had no place to put the hose once she'd removed them.

"Would you like me to put them in my pocket?" he asked.

"I can carry them," she muttered. The idea of handing her intimate undergarment to Blade was embarrassing. How did she get herself into situations like this?

"It's up to you." His eyes were brimming with merriment. "For the record, however, I do know what panty hose look like."

"I'm sure you do," she answered shortly.

The small incident had restored Blade's good humor, at least. He gathered small flat stones and challenged Jessica to see who could skip them farthest over the water as they strolled the length of the beach.

"I didn't realize we'd walked this far," Jessica said, panting when they'd turned around and were halfway home. "It's rough going in this dry sand."

"Let's sit down and rest for a few minutes," he suggested.

They chose a spot where they could prop their backs against a sand dune and gaze out at the ocean. The regular ebb and flow of the water was fascinating to watch.

"I love this place," Blade said quietly. "Just knowing it was here helped me over some bad spots when the going got rugged."

"Was it very terrible?"

"Yes."

The bleakness in his eyes suggested such horrors that Jessica shivered in spite of her sweater.

"You're cold." He started to remove his coat. "Take my jacket."

She stopped him. "I'm fine. I just got a chill for a second."

"Do you want to go back to the house?"

"Not yet. It's so beautiful out here."

"Very beautiful."

The stars reflected points of light in his eyes as he reached out to brush away a strand of hair that had blown across her face. His hand remained like a caress, then trailed down to circle her throat, his thumb resting in the small hollow. The pulsing contact merged with her heartbeat.

She moistened her dry lips. "Perhaps we'd better go in, after all."

"Do you really want to?" When she couldn't answer he said, "I've been wanting to kiss you all evening."

His lips were cool against hers, but they lit a flame in her veins. Jessica shivered again as Blade put his arms around her and gently urged her backward onto the sand. Cradling her against his lean length, he parted her lips for a deep kiss that destroyed her last defense.

His hand caressed her hip in a slow rhythm that was almost unbearably erotic. Only a thin piece of silk separated his hand from her quivering skin.

"You're driving me crazy, Jessica," he muttered against her throat. "You're like a fever in my blood. Do you know how much I want you?"

"Yes," she whispered, feeling the same way.

"I've dreamed about touching you like this."

His hand slipped under the hem of her dress and caressed her bare thigh. When he moved higher to the rounded curve of her hip, Jessica sucked in her breath sharply and tensed with anticipation.

Blade drew the wrong conclusion. He groaned and rolled away from her. "I'm sorry, honey. I just got carried away."

The cold air after the warmth of his body brought Jessica to her senses. "I...it's all right. I understand."

"I wish *I* did. I've been acting like a schoolboy. Why do I do these things?"

Jessica didn't want Blade to get analytical and start remembering that she never put up any objection. "It's merely propinquity," she said hastily. "We see each other every day."

"I see Mrs. Bartlett every day, but I don't try to attack her every time I get her alone."

"Be serious. I'm sure you don't give me a second thought when I'm not around."

"I try not to," he answered grimly.

"Well, thanks a lot!"

"Do you want me to, Jessica?" His eyes were fathomless pools in the darkness.

What did he expect her to say? Yes, I want to have a torrid affair with you on the nights you're not with

Crystal? Blade just admitted he was trying not to get involved with her.

"Certainly not." Jessica forced herself to sound amused. "I've finally found someone who really interests me."

"Meaning Bennington, I suppose," he said evenly.

"Why not? Stewart says he's going to teach me to have fun, and he certainly lives a life I could get used to," she lied.

"I never realized money was so appealing to you."

"Only the wealthy can afford to be indifferent to money." She stood up and brushed sand from her sweater. "I'm going in."

"Go ahead. I'll be along in a little while." Blade's moon-washed features seemed to be carved out of stone.

After that ill-fated night, relations between Jessica and Blade were more strained than they'd ever been. They'd had many sharp clashes before, but both had been secretly anxious to make up. This time was different. He was coolly remote, and she was deeply hurt by his rejection.

To show she didn't care, Jessica accepted all of Stewart's invitations, knowing Blade disapproved. Although why he should care, she couldn't imagine. He saw even more of Crystal. Jessica knew because Blade made a point of keeping her informed.

"I'm taking Crystal to the Black and White Ball tonight," he remarked as he started up the stairs one evening.

"Thank you for sharing that with me," Jessica answered ironically.

"I wanted you to know where to reach me in case an emergency arose with Kevin," he explained patiently.

"Assuming I was here when it happened."

"You can tell Mrs. Bartlett where I'll be."

"Tell her yourself." Jessica stalked into the den.

Jessica wasn't having as good a time with Stewart as she had in the beginning, but she would have allowed herself to be staked to an ant hill before admitting it. She pretended to be enjoying herself, but in addition to her growing boredom, Stewart was becoming increasingly amorous.

Larry wasn't happy with the situation either. "I can't believe Stew would let me down like this," he exclaimed angrily to his sister one afternoon.

"What's the matter. Did he drop Jessica?"

"No, that's the trouble. He thinks he's in love with her."

"She must be giving him some encouragement. Your plan worked. What more do you want?"

"Only half of the problem is solved. I counted on Stew to keep me informed about Blade. If our dear cousin is getting serious with anyone, we're out of the picture."

"What's the news from the home front?"

"That's just it—Stew doesn't know. He refuses to pump Jessica because he doesn't want her to think about Blade when she's with him."

"Your old school chum has more sense than I gave him credit for," Nina said. "He couldn't stand the competition."

"Whose side are you on?" Larry snarled.

"To tell you the truth, I think we're just spinning our wheels. We could never put anything over on Blade when we were kids, and he's gotten a lot smarter since he grew up."

"You're not quitting on me now. We'll get what we need without Stew. You'll call Jessica and get the scoop on Blade."

"I'm glad to see you kept all the difficult chores for yourself," Nina said dryly.

Nina's phone call wasn't welcome, but Jessica tried to be polite. She was curious about the reason for the call, since they'd never pretended to be friendly.

"How are you and Stewart getting along?" Nina asked with a heavy-handed pretense of interest. "He's quite a hunk, isn't he?"

"I suppose you could say so," Jessica answered cautiously, wondering if Stewart had dumped Nina for her.

That didn't seem to be the case since Nina continued enthusiastically. "He's certainly crazy about you. I wouldn't be surprised to get a wedding announcement."

"Don't you think you're being a little premature?"

"Not from the way he's been carrying on to Larry. You were smart to concentrate on Stewart instead of Blade. I don't suppose Blade will ever get married," Nina remarked artlessly.

"That would be to your advantage, wouldn't it?"

"Only if he stays single all year. Which seems like a pretty sure bet. Since he already has more money than he knows what to do with, I don't imagine he'd marry just to get more." Nina's voice ended on a slightly questioning note.

At last Jessica knew the reason for the phone call. "I don't mean to dampen your hopes, but I wouldn't rush to place that bet," she said sweetly. "Blade is out every night with a woman named Crystal Hansen, and he gets that silly look on his face when he talks about her."

"That's characteristic of men in general," Nina said scornfully. "Blade's been in love a hundred times, and he'll be in love a hundred times more."

"That's what I would have thought, given his track record, but he's awfully touchy about Crystal. He's practically not speaking to me right now because he thought I criticized her, and you know what a good relationship we used to have."

"That proves he's infatuated with her, not that he has any long-term plans." The indecision in Nina's voice showed she was trying to convince herself. "Blade won't be around here himself after a year."

"You don't seem to know your cousin very well. Just the other night he told me how much he loves this place. He said he dreamed about it all the time he was overseas."

"I had no idea Blade was considering settling down here," Nina said slowly.

"That could be another indication that he intends to get married." For all she knew, that could be true, Jessica thought bleakly.

"Well, it's been nice talking to you." Nina ended the conversation abruptly.

She was probably anxious to get her report back to Larry, Jessica suspected, without feeling guilty. Maybe she'd embellished the truth a bit, but she hadn't told Nina any outright lies. Besides, the two of them deserved to worry.

Jessica saw very little of Blade for the next few days except at breakfast, where their conversation was kept to a minimum. Other than that, he used his residence as a place to change clothes.

One afternoon, Blade surprised Jessica by storming into her office when he returned from work. He was often in and out of the house before she even knew he'd been there. This particular day he not only sought her out, he had fire in his eyes.

Flinging a piece of paper on her desk he barked out, "Look at this! It's an absolute outrage. Somebody's going to pay dearly for this!"

It was an unsigned poison-pen letter of the vilest sort, detailing sexual indiscretions supposedly committed by Crystal with numerous men. Jessica's stomach churned as she read the disgusting thing.

"The person who wrote this must be sick!" she exclaimed.

He glared at her. "Obviously, but that's no excuse."

"You don't think *I* wrote it?" Jessica was aghast.

"Of course not," he answered impatiently. "I know exactly who's behind this smear campaign—my conniving cousins."

"They're not very pleasant, but surely they wouldn't do anything this vicious."

"Larry and Nina would do anything for money." Blade scowled fiercely. "I have a damn good mind to marry Crystal just to make sure they don't get it."

"That seems a little drastic. Unless it was what you planned anyhow," Jessica couldn't help adding.

"I suppose you're right," he muttered, without answering her implied question. "But I'm not going to let them get away with this. Larry was always a sniveling little weasel, and Nina isn't much better. It's time they got what they deserve."

"What are you going to do?"

"I'd like to pound him into a pulp, but I can't very well do that to her." Blade considered the possibilities with dissatisfaction. "I could take the letter to the postal authorities and tell them who I suspect. They'd prove it in nothing flat. I'd do it, too, if I were sure Crystal wouldn't be dragged into this mess."

"Perhaps it would be better if you talked to Larry and told him the trouble he could be in."

"I don't trust myself to talk to him in my present mood," Blade said darkly. He stared at Jessica, becoming fully aware of her for the first time. "I'm sorry I dumped all this on you. I had to blow off steam or explode."

"I understand," she said quietly.

"It's that damn will!" he burst out, clenching his fists. "It's ruining all our lives."

Jessica couldn't have agreed more. It had certainly altered hers. "At least we have a time limit. We won't be stuck here forever." She tried to look cheerful at the prospect.

"That's one way of looking at it." He stared at her broodingly. "Do you know what you'll do afterward?"

"I haven't really thought about it. Something always turns up."

"You can afford to take time off, perhaps travel. Have you ever been to Europe?"

"No, but I'd like to go, especially to the great capitals. They look so glamorous in posters and brochures."

"Those only show you the tourist attractions. You have to stroll down the streets and mingle with the people. That's how you get to know a city."

The anger drained out of Blade's face and his tension disappeared as he talked about his experiences in various fabled cities. Jessica listened, entranced, almost holding her breath for fear of breaking the bond between them.

"I'd like to show you Europe the way you should see it," he said impulsively.

She gazed at him with shining eyes. "I wish it was possible."

"Anything is possible if you're willing to pay the price." Warring emotions crossed his face as he looked at her.

Jessica could have cried when the phone rang. For the first time in weeks she and Blade were talking spontaneously, but the slightest thing could rupture their fragile rapport. Why did they have to be interrupted just now? She answered the phone reluctantly.

"Hello, dollface. It's the love of your life," Stewart informed her.

"Oh. Hi." Jessica was careful not to say Stewart's name.

"Can you be ready half an hour sooner tonight? I'm on the hospitality committee, and they want us there early." They were going to one of the endless dances at Stewart's country club.

"Sure, no problem," she said, anxious to get rid of him.

Stewart caught her attention with his next remark. "Wear a dress with short sleeves. I bought you something you'll want to show off."

"Another present? You really shouldn't have, Stewart. I—" Too late, Jessica glanced up and saw the damage had been done.

Blade's mouth was curved mockingly. "I guess you already found someone willing to pay the price." He sauntered to the door and raised one hand. "See you around."

Jessica knew exactly what Blade was thinking, but he was wrong. Stewart had tried to urge expensive gifts on her, all of which she'd refused. She was about to do it again, but Blade automatically assumed she was merely being coy. He was convinced she was motivated by money.

In all fairness, she had gone out of her way to give him that impression on a couple of occasions, but he should have realized it was only out of annoyance. Blade should know her better by now.

Jessica's wretchedness turned to anger. If he could think she was such a shallow, grasping person, they didn't even have the basis for a friendship. As far as she was concerned, the cold war was back on!

Stewart considered the pursuit of pleasure a full-time job. But since Jessica already had a job, she was frequently exhausted. She longed to stay home occasionally and go to bed early with a good book, a luxury she denied herself. If Blade could work all day and stay out half the night, so could she. He wasn't going to find her sitting home alone.

Mrs. Bartlett finally expressed concern. "How long are you going to keep up this pace? You and Mr. Blade should really slow down a little. He looks terrible, and you're as thin as a rail."

"Thin is in," Jessica told her lightly.

"In the hospital is where you'll be," the older woman predicted darkly.

"I'm fine, really." Jessica edged toward the kitchen door. "I just came to tell you I won't be home for dinner tonight."

"So what else is new? Neither of you ever are anymore. I don't know what you need me for," the housekeeper grumbled.

Jessica tried to jolly her out of it. "Who would make Kevin every little thing his heart desires? You spoil him terribly."

"Somebody has to. The poor little thing eats his dinner in front of the TV every night because he doesn't have anybody to talk to."

"He's probably the envy of every kid in school," Jessica answered as she went out the door.

Jessica's complacency was shattered when Kevin came home from school the next afternoon. He handed her his report card with a touch of defiance, and she soon discovered the reason for it.

"This isn't a very good report card, Kevin. All of your grades have slipped." When he didn't answer, she asked, "Is the work too hard for you?"

"No." He seemed unconcerned.

"Then why have your grades gone down?"

"Sometimes I didn't do my homework."

"Why not?"

He shrugged. "I didn't feel like it."

Jessica looked at him in perplexity. This wasn't at all like Kevin. "If the teacher assigns homework you have to do it, even if you don't feel like it. Everybody has to do things they don't want to do."

"You and Uncle Blade don't," he answered stubbornly.

"Whatever gave you that idea?"

"You go out every night having fun."

"I wouldn't exactly call it fun. We work hard all day, and we need a little relaxation," she explained carefully. "Adults might seem to have more freedom, but when we were your age we had to follow the rules just like you do."

"What difference does it make if I get *A*'s or *C*'s? Nobody cares anyway."

"How can you say that?"

"Because it's true. You're never here, and he isn't either."

Her heart sank when she heard Kevin revert to calling his uncle "he." Mrs. Bartlett's words suddenly registered, and Jessica was conscience-stricken. How long had it been since they'd spent any time with Kevin? Blade was too busy with his girlfriend, and she was wasting her time just to spite him. In their preoccupation with themselves, they'd forgotten about a little boy who needed them.

Blade might be too far gone to care but she wasn't. Jessica looked at Kevin sternly. "From now on, young man, you're going to do your homework, and I'll be here to see that you do—starting tonight."

Hope filled his face. "You're not going out?"

"I was, but this is more important. Sit right there while I make a phone call."

Stewart showed his displeasure when she broke their date. "But I have fifth-row center seats to the theater."

"I'm sure you can get someone to go with you."

"Why can't you go?"

"I have to help Kevin with his homework," she said truthfully. "And incidentally, I'll have to cancel out for the weekend, too."

"Since when do kids go to school on the weekend?"

"We're going to make some field trips."

"Are you giving me the brush-off?" Stewart demanded.

Jessica sighed. "Please don't put it that way. I've enjoyed our time together, Stewart. You showed me a whole new world, but it isn't one I can live in."

"I don't get it. How can you say you had fun, but you don't want to see me anymore?"

She glanced over at Kevin. "I don't think I could explain it in a way you'd understand."

"Oh, I understand, all right! It's Blade, isn't it? You were just using me to make him jealous, and your strategy finally worked."

"I said you wouldn't understand. Goodbye, Stewart."

Jessica dismissed him from her mind as soon as she hung up. All she felt was a sense of relief.

"Okay, get your books, and let's start working on those grades," she told Kevin.

"Can't we do it after dinner? I haven't taken King for his walk yet. Uncle Blade said I have to be responsible," he reminded her craftily.

"How come you only remember when it suits your purpose?" She laughed. "All right, King has priority, but tonight we hit the books."

"Will Uncle Blade be home for dinner?"

"I doubt it, but we don't need him." When that sounded too harsh she said, "I mean, you're going to do the actual work, and it only takes one of us to crack the whip."

"I liked it when we did things together," he said wistfully. "Do you think we can again?"

"Well, I . . . it's a possibility." Jessica didn't see fit to tell him the difference between possibility and probability.

She and Kevin took King for a run on the beach, and then went up to his room to listen to a new tape he wanted her to hear. While he was looking for it in his extensive collection, Jessica sat on the floor with King between her knees, brushing his thick coat. The formerly roly-poly puppy was already growing into a big dog.

When the stereo started to blast Jessica winced. "Does it have to be that loud?"

"You got to hear it."

"People across the bay in Oakland can hear it," she complained, but she didn't make him turn it down.

The noise drowned out Blade's approach. He stood in the doorway for several moments, watching them with an indefinable expression on his face until they finally noticed him.

"Isn't the music a little loud?" he asked.

His tone had been mild, but Jessica took immediate offense. Was that all he could do, criticize? "All the kids play their music this way. You're just out of touch," she said disdainfully.

Blade's face darkened. "I didn't realize I was so old. Maybe I'd better totter out of here while I can still navigate."

"Uncle Blade, wait!" Kevin stopped him. "Can you have dinner with Jessica and me tonight?"

Blade looked at her mockingly. "No date with Bennington this evening? Don't tell me the world-class playboy can't keep up the pace."

Jessica was about to snap back something equally sarcastic when she thought better of it. The uncertain expression on Kevin's face showed he was picking up the bad vibes between them.

She directed her answer to the boy. "I forgot to tell Mrs. Bartlett. Will you go down and ask her to set another place?"

"You didn't answer my question," Blade persisted after the child had left the room. "Is there a rift in the romance?"

"If you paid attention to anyone but yourself, you'd know that Kevin is feeling neglected," she answered crisply. "He's been left on his own for weeks, and as a way of striking back he let his grades slip."

Blade was clearly caught off base. "We have breakfast together every morning."

"Big deal. Twenty minutes out of a whole day."

"I didn't realize," he said slowly.

"Neither did I until I scolded him about his report card, and he said nobody cared anyway."

Blade groaned. "He said that? You're right, I've been criminally negligent."

She couldn't help relenting at his obvious remorse. "I wasn't watching the store either, but no permanent damage has been done. Kevin bounced right back when I told him I was staying home tonight."

"You broke a date for him, didn't you?"

She shrugged. "It wasn't a huge sacrifice. I was getting tired of the rat race anyway."

"You continually put me to shame, Jessica," he said huskily.

She didn't intend to be suckered by his bogus gratitude again. "I didn't do it for you, I did it for Kevin."

"I realize that," he answered gravely.

Kevin returned. "Mrs. Bartlett says she's glad you finally came to your senses."

"Would you mind making another trip downstairs to tell her that I did, too?" Blade asked. "Tell her there will be three of us for dinner."

"Oh, boy! Super!" Kevin wheeled around and ran down the hall.

"You didn't have to do that," Jessica said. "One of us is enough."

The lines had smoothed out of Blade's face. "Why should you have all the fun?"

"I'm sure you could have more fun following your original plans," she replied primly.

"Is that what you think?" He smiled.

Kevin returned once more, out of breath and looking anxious. "Did you tell him?" he asked Jessica.

"Tell me what?" Blade asked.

"About my report card."

"I had to tell him," she said.

"Are you mad at me?" Kevin asked his uncle.

"No, I'm not angry," Blade said gently. "I would like to see you get those grades up, though."

"I will, I promise!"

"Okay. Then we can talk about something else. Tomorrow is Saturday. How would you like to go ice-skating?"

"I don't know how," the child said regretfully.

"Then it's time you learned. Your father and I used to spend some great Saturdays at the rink, picking up girls. But I guess you're too young for that," Blade teased.

"I'll be eleven soon." Kevin was anxious to measure up to whatever his uncle wanted of him.

"It's clearly time you completed your education. If we can persuade Jessica to go with us, she can hold you up on one side, and I'll take the other."

"I'd be delighted to go along, but I won't be any help," she said. "I never learned to skate, either."

"I'm part of an underprivileged family," Blade exclaimed.

Dinner that night was like a party. Mrs. Bartlett outdid herself in the culinary department, and Blade took over the entertainment. They lingered at the table much longer than usual, enjoying each other's company.

After dinner Blade and Jessica went back to Kevin's room to supervise while he did his homework. The simple lessons didn't take long.

When he was almost finished Jessica stood up and stretched. "You two can carry on without me. I'm going to bed."

"So early?" Blade asked with a shadow of disappointment. "It's only nine o'clock."

"I've been promising myself an early night. See you both in the morning."

Jessica really was tired, but that wasn't the reason. Quite simply, she didn't want to be alone with Blade. Nothing good ever came of it. They had joined forces temporarily for Kevin's sake, but she had no illusions that their goodwill would last. She was through hoping and dreaming.

Jessica had planned to sit and watch while Blade taught Kevin to skate, but he wouldn't hear of it.

"How are you going to teach both of us at once, when neither of us can stand up alone?" she asked after they got to the ice rink.

"I've hired an instructor for Kevin. He won't feel as awkward with a stranger as he would with me."

She looked over at the youngster who was completely absorbed in lacing up his skates. "He's so anxious for your approval."

"I know," Blade answered in a muted voice. "I'm a very lucky man."

Jessica almost met with disaster the minute she stepped onto the ice. Her ankles felt like cooked spaghetti, and the ice was alarmingly slick. Blade started out holding her hand, but when her feet threatened to fly out from under her, he put an arm firmly around her waist.

"Easy does it. Just glide," he instructed. "Pretend you're waltzing."

"My generation never waltzed, and if this is what it's like, I know why," she gasped.

"Little kids can do it," he scoffed. "Look at them."

It was true. Small children were whirling around the rink like pros. "I feel so clumsy," she complained.

"All beginners do. You'll get the hang of it. You're naturally graceful."

"Your standards must be different from everyone else's," she muttered, grabbing his hand as she lurched awkwardly.

He laughed. "Well, maybe you're not exactly a sylph at the moment."

"Don't you dare make fun of me," she ordered.

"What are you going to do about it?" he teased. "I finally have you completely in my power."

Swinging her around to face him, Blade put his arms around her and skated backward. His support kept her from falling, but she leaned heavily against him, completely off balance. The enforced contact made her aware of the strength of his body. His supple muscles absorbed her weight easily, moving in perfect coordination in spite of her inert body.

"Blade, stop!" she protested. "You're just dragging me along. This isn't teaching me to skate."

"No, but it's a lot more fun." He slowed to a stop.

Jessica's arms were clasped tightly around his chest. Every time she tried to let go, her feet slid and she was forced to cling to him again. She was indeed powerless if he refused to take her over to the railing.

"Please, Blade," she said appealingly.

His breath caught as he gazed into her upturned, pleading face. They both felt the change in mood. The light teasing had vanished, replaced by the desire that exploded so inexplicably between them at an instant's notice. A current seemed to flow between them, fusing their bodies magnetically.

Blade broke the contact. Guiding her over to the edge he said, "Okay, you can rest for a few minutes."

He skated off by himself, speed racing around the rink as though in need of physical release. Jessica watched his superb performance with admiration. Blade's emotions might give him trouble, but he was in complete charge of his magnificent body.

Chapter Eight

Jessica didn't learn to ice skate that day, but Kevin did. After his lesson he made them watch while he lurched proudly around the rink by himself. The awkwardness Blade and Jessica had felt together after the incident on the ice was completely dispelled as they watched the little boy together.

"He's a really terrific kid," Jessica said with a softened expression. "I couldn't be prouder if he were my own."

"I feel the same way." Blade reached out for her hand, but it was the hand of friendship, and she had no reservations about accepting it.

That evening they had dinner at a pizza parlor, Kevin's choice. Then they went to a movie. When they got home, the little boy was drooping. He went to bed without protest.

As Jessica was following him upstairs, Blade stopped her. "You're not going to bed early again?"

"It's been a full day."

"Not the kind you would have spent with Bennington. Do you mind not seeing him this weekend, Jessica?"

Blade didn't know she'd broken up with Stewart, and Jessica wasn't about to tell him. "No more than you do about breaking your dates with Crystal. It was all in a good cause. Good night, Blade."

She left him at the foot of the stairs, watching until she was out of sight.

They all slept late the next morning. Since Mrs. Bartlett was off on Sunday, Jessica expected to cook breakfast, but Blade took them out instead.

Jessica ordered strawberries and cream, a stack of pancakes and a side order of sausages. The portions were large, but she finished everything on her plate.

"I don't know how you can eat like that and keep your figure," Blade remarked in disbelief.

"You can't win." She sighed. "Mrs. Bartlett told me I'm too thin, and you're telling me I'm going to get fat."

"Not at all. I admire a woman with a healthy appetite. There's nothing worse than taking someone out for a meal and having her pick at the food because she's on a diet."

Jessica realized she'd been guilty of that herself the past weeks. Stewart had taken her to the finest restaurants, but she'd never had any appetite.

"I've never had to diet, but I feel sorry for people who do," she said. "It must be hard to deny yourself something you really want."

"Tell me about it," he answered sardonically.

When she glanced up quickly Blade was signaling the waiter for the check.

They went to the zoo that afternoon at Kevin's request, and although they started out together, he soon raced ahead. Jessica and Blade strolled along behind, stopping for a more leisurely look at the animals.

"Isn't he magnificent?" she asked, gazing at a majestic Bengal tiger pacing around his cement grotto. "How could anyone shoot something that beautiful for no good reason?"

"It's called sport," Blade answered dryly. "Tigers are so endangered that soon the only ones left might be in zoos."

"I know it's for their survival, but I still feel sad to see one penned up. He shouldn't be in a concrete compound in San Francisco. He should be roaming the jungles of India, free.

"Ideally, everyone should be able to do what they want, but that isn't always the case," he replied, staring at the restless animal.

Was Blade equating himself with the tiger? Did he feel just as trapped? "Unlike animals, people control their own destinies," she pointed out.

"Perhaps cavemen did, although they had their problems with dinosaurs and such. But modern man complicated his life when he invented money."

"Not necessarily. Money can be used for research, for improving the quality of life, for funding the arts, any number of worthwhile things."

"It can also bring out the baser qualities in people," Blade said somberly.

"I suppose you're referring to Larry and Nina."

His features sharpened. "The obvious ones aren't a threat."

Jessica slanted a covert glance at his austere profile. Was he beginning to question the reason for Crystal's devotion? Anything that kept him from marrying that man-eater should be encouraged.

"I can understand why someone in your position would feel that way," she remarked casually. "A lot of women would do almost anything to marry you."

"I'm aware of that, but what do I do about it?"

"Keep it in mind," she advised succinctly.

He turned his head to look at her. "Suppose I fell in love? How could I ever be sure?"

If Blade was truly in love with Crystal and not simply having a heated affair, it was a lost cause. Jessica sighed. "I guess you'll have to trust your own judgment."

His expression was unreadable. "That's the best advice you can give anyone. Come on, let's get some peanuts."

Blade offered to take them out to dinner that night, but neither Jessica nor Kevin were very enthusiastic about the idea.

"Mrs. Bartlett has a whole freezer full of food. Why don't I make dinner at home?" she asked.

Kevin seconded the notion. "I want to watch a movie. Can I have my dinner in front of the TV?"

Jessica and Blade looked at each other in wry amusement. "For this we gave up our weekend?" Blade asked.

Jessica was hurt to find out the way he really felt. She'd foolishly thought Blade was having a good time. Turning her back to look in the freezer she said, "It's still early. You can give Crystal a call. Maybe she hasn't made other plans."

"That wouldn't be fair. Why don't you call Bennington instead? Kevin is my responsibility."

"I wish you'd stop saying that!" she exclaimed angrily. "Just because you're his uncle doesn't mean you care about him and I don't. You can care deeply for someone without being related."

"That's certainly true," he commented wryly. "I'm sorry, Jessica. I was only trying to salvage at least part of your ruined weekend."

"By pushing me onto Stewart?" Her quick temper exploded. It had been a glorious weekend until then. "For your information, I'm not seeing him anymore."

"He was that upset over a few broken dates?" Blade asked incredulously.

"No, it was my idea."

"I thought you were enjoying life in the fast lane," he said slowly. "Why did you dump him, Jessica?"

"I'd rather not discuss it. Go in the other room and watch television while I get dinner on," she ordered.

A smile broke out on his face, chasing away all the tension lines. "Can I stay in here with you if I promise not to mention his name again?"

"It's no big deal." She shrugged. "Now that you know I'm not giving up anything, you can call Crystal with a clear conscience."

"If you're trying to get rid of me, it won't work. What can I do to help?"

"Do you know anything about cooking?" Jessica looked dubiously at a casserole of frozen chicken and dumplings. "Do I heat this on top of the stove, or in the oven?"

"You put it in the microwave if you expect to have dinner any time soon."

"I don't know how to use one."

"You have surprising gaps in your education," he observed.

"It's not my fault. My mother cooked the old-fashioned way. We didn't have a microwave oven when I was growing up."

"Possibly because they weren't invented yet."

"That would have made it harder to learn," she agreed.

Blade was more knowledgeable in the kitchen. He was the one who made the salad and warmed the biscuits.

When she remarked that he was doing all the work he said, "You can put the dishes in the dishwasher later. I assume you know how to use that."

"No. We ate off paper plates and threw them away afterward," she said mischievously.

The tension between them had completely disappeared. They prepared dinner together, joking with the ease of old friends. Or like a happily married couple, Jessica thought wistfully.

The impression heightened as they ate together at the kitchen table, talking about plans for the coming week.

After the dishes were cleared, they joined Kevin in the den. But when it was time for the youngster to go to bed, Jessica was reluctant to follow him upstairs as she'd intended. It wasn't difficult for Blade to persuade her to stay.

"You're not going to leave me alone again?" he asked plaintively.

"We've been together all day," she said hesitantly.

"Without a serious argument." He laughed. "Are you afraid to press your luck?"

"Well, our détente has been known to end with a bang."

"Not tonight, I promise. Do you play chess? We couldn't possibly argue while we're concentrating on a game."

"I'm pretty rusty. I haven't played in a long time."

"Good. Then I'll have a chance to beat you."

Blade would have won anyway. He was a superb player who made his moves in a minimum of time. Jessica had to deliberate over hers. She studied the board for long minutes, unaware that Blade wasn't plotting his strategy. He was gazing at her with a softened expression on his face.

After she'd been checkmated Blade started to set up the board for another game, but Jessica stopped him.

"Don't you want a chance to get even?" he asked.

"I couldn't beat you if we played for a week."

"I'll let you win," he coaxed.

"No thanks. When I win it will be on the up-and-up. That's the only way I play."

"I'm beginning to find that out," he said admiringly.

Jessica stood, feeling suddenly constrained. "I . . . uh . . . guess I'll see you in the morning."

He smiled. "That's a safe bet."

"Today was fun. I haven't been to the zoo in ages." Jessica wondered why she was dragging things out. They'd had a pleasant evening without friction. The sensible thing to do was say good-night. But she felt a curious reluctance.

"You were the one who made the day special." He drew nearer.

The light in Blade's eyes gave her the impetus to end the evening. "Will you turn out the lights? I'm going to bed."

"Wait, Jessica. I haven't thanked you yet for getting Kevin back on the track."

"You know I was glad to do it."

"I'm sorry I implied you didn't care. I was way out of line. You're the kindest, most caring woman I've ever known."

"Kevin makes it easy to be," she mumbled.

"I wish you felt that way about the whole family," he said huskily.

She tried to defuse the potentially dangerous situation by saying jokingly, "I can't get excited about your relatives."

"How about just me?"

"Why do you continue to do this, Blade?" she asked in frustration. "We always wind up barely speaking to each other. It's almost as though you enjoy being on the outs."

"That's the last thing I want," he answered fervently. "You're right, as usual. Go to bed before I do something stupid." He framed her face in his palms and gazed at her tenderly. "Good night, sweet Jessica."

His lips touched hers gently. It was a kiss given in friendship and gratitude, without any hint of lust. But no kiss between them could remain dispassionate. Jessica was rooted to the spot, incapable of moving. She stared up at him, noticing inconsequential things—how long and thick his eyelashes were, the square jaw that gave his face character.

He stared at her in the same way for a quivering moment that built in intensity. Then he lowered his head, almost in slow motion. His mouth covered hers again, only this time with naked hunger.

Jessica remained passive for only an instant. When his tongue parted her lips, she put her arms around his neck and closed the small distance between them. Blade's response was immediate. He pulled her so close that their bodies were molded together at every point.

"I can't leave you alone," he groaned, tangling his fingers in her hair. "I've tried, but it's no use."

"I know," she whispered.

His eyes blazed as he stared down at her lambent face. "You want me, too, don't you, sweetheart?"

"Yes." How could she deny what was so evident?

He pulled her head back and strung a line of kisses down her throat. "Why have we been fighting this when it's so right?"

Jessica made a valiant effort to resist his potent allure. She had reacted instinctively to his kiss, but now was the time to call a halt, before they did something they'd both regret.

"It *isn't* right, Blade. Desire isn't enough—for me, at least. I don't want to be a casual incident in your life."

"Casual?" He stared at her incredulously. "Do you know the sleepless nights I've spent tormented by the thought of you, just across the hall? I wanted to come over and share your bed. I kept thinking about how your body would feel, all soft and warm."

Jessica braced her palms against his chest as he tried to urge her nearer. "That's only because we're living too close together. I told you that before. Why won't you admit it?"

"Because it isn't true. Tell me you don't want me, but don't tell me I don't want you."

His hand cupped her breast and his thumb rotated over her erect nipple. Jessica drew in her breath sharply as his tongue continued the erotic seduction, tracing the inner curves of her ear before dipping into the small cavity.

She dug her nails into his forearms, trying to summon the willpower to stop him. But when his hands slipped inside her jeans and stroked her buttocks in a sensual pattern, she gave up the struggle. Clasping her arms around his neck once more, she sought his mouth blindly.

"My little darling," he exulted. "You're going to be mine, aren't you?"

When he grasped the hem of her sweater she said, "Not here. Let's go upstairs."

"No, here," he said firmly, stripping off her sweater before she could stop him. "I won't let you have second thoughts. This was meant to be."

As she started to argue he unhooked her bra. Jessica's protests were forgotten when Blade's fingertips feathered tantalizingly over her breasts. The light in his eyes as he gazed at her seminude body was dazzling. Jessica was transfixed as he unzipped her jeans. They slid down her hips to the floor and she stepped out of them, holding Blade's outstretched arms. She was left with only a pair of sheer panties.

Clasping her shoulders lightly he lowered his head to kiss each breast, then circled first one rosy tip, then the other with his tongue. The sensation was exquisite.

"You're as beautiful as I knew you would be," he murmured.

Her legs felt boneless when he slipped a forefinger inside the elastic of her panties and eased them down her thighs. Kneeling before her, he wrapped his arms around her hips and kissed the soft skin of her stomach.

As his mouth trailed lower, Jessica clutched at his shoulders. "I didn't know it could be like this," she gasped.

He looked up with incandescent eyes. "You're the one who makes it special. Every inch of you is enchanting."

His mouth was like a burning torch igniting her. Jessica's legs finally gave way and she sank to her knees facing him. Her hands were shaking as she pulled his jersey over his broad shoulders. Blade caught her urgency. With rapid motions he tore open his jeans. While he was wriggling out of them, Jessica pushed him backward onto the carpet. He carried her with him and their bodies made naked contact for the first time.

Blade's legs scissored around hers, locking their bodies even closer. She was a willing prisoner. Scattering frantic kisses over his face, she moved sensuously against him.

"Sweet, passionate Jessica," he groaned. "You're driving me over the edge."

Wrapping his arms around her he rolled over, parting her legs with his knee. Jessica accepted him into the core of her being with a jubilation that matched his own. Their ardor mounted with every movement, every fevered caress until it reached dizzying heights. A final burst of sensation jolted through their bodies, then gradually diminished to a pulsing satisfaction.

After they'd drifted into a peaceful state, Blade touched her hair lovingly. "Have I told you that you're wonderful?"

She smiled. "You inspired me."

"Wait until you see what else I have planned."

She traced the curve of his generous mouth. "I don't think you could top yourself."

"Let's hear what you have to say after a couple of months."

His teasing words forced her back to reality. Jessica's smile faded. "Aren't you forgetting something?"

"What do you mean?"

"Your commitment to Crystal. I'm not blaming you for what happened tonight. It was as much my fault as yours, but that doesn't make it right."

She tried to move away, but his arms tightened. "If you think I'd let you go now, you're out of your mind."

"I expected higher ethics from you," she said tautly. Did Blade really believe he could have it all?

He raised up on one elbow to look directly at her. "I won't try to pretend that Crystal and I were merely friends, but there was no understanding between us."

"I'll bet she'd tell you differently."

"I've given her no reason to." He paused to choose his words with care. "Crystal was an obvious choice when I stopped railing against my lot and decided to make a life for myself here. Slipping into her world of ceaseless activity was just what I needed at the time. But it was never my kind of world. I made no secret of that."

Jessica was unconvinced. "Women have been known to change their life-style for the man they love."

"Crystal doesn't love me." He made a wry face. "She likes being seen with me because I'm considered a catch, but if someone more noteworthy came along she'd drop me in a flash. I have no illusions about that."

"Doesn't it bother you?"

"Not in the slightest."

"How could you stand to be with someone that shallow?" Jessica exclaimed.

He grinned. "It was starting to wear me down, but I was hoping my perseverance would pay off."

"I don't understand."

"You disliked Crystal so much. I hoped it was because you were jealous."

"You gave her the star treatment to make *me* jealous?" she asked indignantly.

"I was a basketcase when it didn't seem to be working. After you started going with Bennington I almost lost hope."

Jessica was reluctant to admit that her motives were the same as Blade's. It was premature to disclose her love for him, since he hadn't made a similar declaration.

"I knew you didn't like Stewart, but I didn't think you were jealous," she said cautiously.

"That doesn't begin to describe it! I wanted to wipe that self-satisfied smirk off his face permanently. That's why I tried to be out when he came to call for you."

She laughed helplessly. "Would you say we suffered from a lack of communication?"

"I suffered, all right. You asked me, now I'll ask you. How could you stand him night after night?"

"He took me to interesting places and showered me with attention," she answered carefully. "It was the kind of life I'd only read about."

"You enjoyed that enough to put up with him?

Jessica was so intent on hiding her true feelings that she didn't notice Blade had become very still. "It was compensation enough for a while."

"You would have gone on seeing him if it hadn't been for Kevin," he said in a flat tone of voice.

"Maybe for a while, out of inertia. But sooner or later boredom would have achieved the same result."

"Would tonight have given you the necessary push?" His eyes kindled at the memory.

"You've definitely taken my mind off Stewart," she answered impishly.

"Perhaps I'd better make sure."

The point of his tongue traced the line of her smiling lips until they opened. Plunging deeply, he explored the moist cavity until Jessica's body throbbed to life.

They made love more leisurely this time, drawing out the incomparable pleasure. Moving languorously they explored every erogenous zone until the hot tide of passion became more compelling. As their desire rose they rode the wild waves together, climbing to the crest in a final explosion of power.

Afterward they relaxed in each other's arms completely sated. Long minutes passed while they simply gloried in a sense of well-being.

Jessica stirred first. "It must be terribly late. We should go to bed."

"I don't want to move until morning," Blade murmured.

"I know, but we have to." She eluded his determined embrace.

"I suppose you're right." He chuckled wickedly, getting to his feet. "How would you explain this to Hawkins and Mrs. B. if they found us here?"

"I'd tell them you seduced me shamelessly."

He clasped his arms around her waist and gazed down at her. "Did I?"

"What do you think?" Her lips brushed his in a butterfly caress.

When they reached the upper hallway Blade followed Jessica into her room.

"You have to go to bed," she scolded.

"That's what I intend doing." He grinned. Over Jessica's objections he slid into her bed and pulled her after him. "Just a few minutes to fulfill my frustrated fantasies," he coaxed.

A few minutes stretched into almost an hour as they kissed and talked softly. Then Blade's gentle fondling grew more sensual, and they made love again. It was almost daylight before he reluctantly went back to his own room.

"I'll have breakfast with Kevin," he said from the doorway. "I want you to sleep late."

"I just might do that." She yawned, feeling completely at peace.

Life was so glorious after that night that Jessica was almost afraid some disaster lay ahead. Nothing could remain this perfect.

It did, though. Outside of the frustration of having to keep their relationship hidden, she and Blade were idyllically happy. They spent every free moment together and made love at every opportunity.

Their feelings weren't as secret as they thought. Mrs. Bartlett might not have guessed the extent of their involvement, but she could tell they were in love. Anyone could. It showed in every glance they exchanged, every casual touch. The older woman was delighted. She had grown fond of Jessica and knew Kevin had, too.

"This house would be perfect for a wedding," she remarked, not very subtly to Jessica one day. "The living room is plenty big for a reception, or we could hold it out back in the garden."

"Doesn't the bride's family give the wedding?" Jessica asked innocently. "This household is strictly male."

"Except for you." The housekeeper gave her an equally innocent look.

"Unfortunately, nobody has asked me to marry him," Jessica answered lightly.

Mrs. Bartlett nodded confidently. "He will."

Jessica didn't want to let her assume something that was by no means certain. She was afraid to even think about it herself. Blade was a tender and masterful lover, but he'd never said those fateful three words.

"If you're talking about Blade and me, you've gotten the wrong idea," she said evenly. "We've become good friends, but marriage is probably out of the question. I mean, it *is* out of the question," she corrected herself hastily. "Blade is a confirmed bachelor."

"There's no such thing. A confirmed bachelor is only a man who hasn't found the right woman yet," Mrs. Bartlett said complacently.

"What makes you think he has now? Blade's been in love with dozens of women."

"Or thought he was."

"We're both saying the same thing." Jessica sighed.

"You don't know Mr. Blade the way I do. He was always a devil with the ladies. They used to call up here day and night. I saw him get interested in one or the other, but it never lasted."

"Aren't you jumping to conclusions, then?" Jessica asked in a small voice. "Blade and I have only been... friendly... for a short time."

"I could tell it was different between you two from the day you moved in."

"We had some terrible arguments in the beginning," Jessica protested.

The older woman chuckled. "That was one indication. Mr. Blade never cared enough to argue with the others. But when you and he were mixing it up, he wasn't fit to live with."

"Naturally he was upset," Jessica said doubtfully. "You have to get along with the people you see every day. Otherwise it's pure hell."

Mrs. Bartlett patted her hand. "Maybe it wasn't my place to say anything, but you be sure and give me plenty of warning before you set the date. I want to get this place in apple-pie order."

Jessica wandered into the den in a daze. Did the housekeeper really have special insight into Blade's emotions? She'd known him for a long time. Was he really acting differently? Was marriage a possibility?

That night Jessica was especially ardent. Blade was enchanted by her passionate response. He brought her rapture that managed to transcend what they'd experienced before. But he didn't say he loved her.

Larry and Nina found out about their affair eventually. Her rift with Stewart gave them the first indication.

"Stew says Jessica called it quits," Larry reported to his sister. "Can you imagine any broad being that dumb?"

"I can't imagine him admitting he got dumped," she answered dryly.

"He wasn't happy about it, I'll tell you. He only told me after I kept bugging him to find out what she knew about Blade."

"You were smart to stay away from Blade yourself. That anonymous letter was a real bomb. How could you do anything that stupid?"

"I don't notice you doing anything constructive," he sneered.

"You call that constructive? Any idiot would know he'd recognize your bumbling trademark. You're just lucky your mail isn't being rerouted to the local lockup."

"Blade was only bluffing," he muttered.

"He won't be if you don't stop playing Machiavelli. I never saw anybody so rotten at it," she said disgustedly. "You'd probably sign your name to a ransom note."

"Will you knock it off?" he asked furiously. "I've had enough of your lip. At least I'm trying to salvage our inheritance. What are you doing?"

"Bowing to the inevitable. Why don't you simply let things take their course? They will anyway."

"That's a defeatist attitude. Didn't I get Jessica away from Blade? I might have broken up *his* romance, too. The trouble is, we don't know."

"Didn't you get a clue from the way he threatened you over that letter about Crystal?"

"Not necessarily. Some of the mud has to stick. Whether he likes it or not, Blade's going to think about those things I wrote. If he questions Crystal about them, it could provoke a hell of an argument. What we have to find out is whether love's sweet song hit a sour note."

"You're in no position to ask him. He'd swat you like a fly."

"I'm not afraid of Blade," Larry blustered.

"Okay. Can I have your car when you're gone?" Nina asked mockingly.

"Will you be serious?" His face darkened with irritation. "I realize I can't get anything out of Blade, but you can."

"No way," she said promptly. "I'm just a little more tolerable to him than you are, but that's like saying a fractured ankle is preferable to a broken leg."

Larry grudgingly had to admit the truth of her statement. "You'll have to tackle Jessica, then."

"I'm not on *her* list of all-time favorites, either."

"You're not trying to win a popularity contest," he said impatiently. "Call her and see if you can find out what Blade is up to."

Nina's telephone conversation with Jessica didn't net the desired information. Jessica parried all of her roundabout questions, and Nina couldn't ask direct ones. She didn't even find out the reason for Jessica's breakup with Stewart. She did try, even though it didn't seem important.

"I was certainly surprised to hear you weren't going with Stewart anymore," was the way Nina began.

"I suppose so, since you had us married and the parents of two point five children, the national average," Jessica answered with amusement.

"Well, he certainly had the hots for you. I didn't think you'd be crazy enough to turn him down. Stew is loaded."

"So I gathered," Jessica replied neutrally.

"Blade doesn't turn you on, and you're not impressed by Stew. What kind of guy *are* you looking for?"

"Actually, I'm not looking for a man." That was certainly true. Jessica had found the perfect one.

"I thought romance was catching. Doesn't Blade's hot and heavy affair make you want to get in the game? He *is* still going with that girl—what was her name? Crystal?"

"That's her name," Jessica answered without embellishment.

Nina gritted her teeth and glared at the phone. It pained her to adopt a sweet tone, an effort at any time. "Did you say he was still going with her?"

"You'd have to ask him. I'm just an employee around here."

"Come on, Jessica! You live in the house. You know what's going on." Nina's impatience got the better of her.

"I mind my own business," Jessica said crisply, tiring of the cat-and-mouse game.

"Meaning I should do the same?" Nina asked dangerously.

"I didn't say that, but it's good advice for anyone. If you want information about Blade, I'd suggest you go to the source. I can't help you."

Nina was fuming when she hung up. She called Jessica a few choice names, and thought of some more for Larry, the clown prince. This was absolutely the last time she'd let him talk her into making a fool of herself. There had to be a better way to get information.

Nina's eyes grew thoughtful. After a few moments she pulled out the telephone directory and then dialed a number.

When Crystal answered Nina said, "This is the society editor at the Journal. I'm doing an item in my column about the Art Association party at the DeYoung Museum last Tuesday, and I'd like to include your name. I was told your escort was Blade Dunsmuir. Is that correct?"

"No, it is *not* correct," Crystal snapped. "I wasn't even at that party, but I'll give you an item for your column. Blade and I have split."

"What a pity. You were such a handsome couple." Nina's voice was syrupy. "Is there a chance you'll get back together? Just between us, of course. I'll keep it in the strictest confidence if you say so."

"In the strictest confidence," Crystal mimicked sarcastically, "I wouldn't take him back on a platter with an apple in his mouth. He and his little secretary deserve each other!"

Nina's happy smile disappeared. "Jessica Lawrence?" she asked sharply.

"That's the one. How do you know her?" Crystal asked suspiciously. "She's scarcely part of the crowd you write about in your column."

Nina hung up unceremoniously, her mind working overtime. The phone rang, startling her.

"Well, what did you find out?" Larry's voice greeted her. "I hope you didn't blow it this time."

Her mouth curved sardonically. "Which do you want first, the good news or the bad news?"

"Stop being a comedian and tell me."

"Blade isn't seeing Crystal anymore. He dropped her for Jessica."

After a moment's shocked surprise, Larry swore viciously. "That conniving little tramp! She used Stew to make Blade jealous."

"Nice going, Brother. You played right into her hand."

"How the hell could I know she was that tricky?"

"You should have recognized the trait, except that she's also smart."

Larry was too devastated to snap back. "The question is, how serious are they?"

"If she's clever enough to lay out a campaign and get him away from another woman who's a pretty hot number, I'd say we were in big trouble."

"Do you think he's considering marriage?" Larry asked.

"I think she'll see to it that the subject comes up a lot."

"We have to do something!"

"I wouldn't advise another poison-pen letter, and I'm not making any more phone calls," Nina stated positively.

"The least you can do is help. I'm doing this for the whole family."

"Then let them do some of the dirty work," Nina said.

"You're a genius!" he shouted jubilantly. "Why didn't I think of that?"

"What did I think of?"

"We'll get Mother to call Blade and warn him about fortune hunters. She's good at that."

"I think she took a course in college," Nina agreed. "It's called, Giving People Advice They Don't Want To Hear."

Larry ignored her, intent on his plan. "Blade can push us around, but he can't be rude to his aunt. He'll have to listen, and some of it's bound to sink in. He knows all that money makes him a target. Jessica can keep bringing up marriage all she wants. It could even work to our advantage. If we can start him wondering about her motives, we might be able to salvage this thing yet."

"You could be right for once in your life," Nina said thoughtfully.

Chapter Nine

Jessica and Blade were unaware of the scheming going on behind their backs. Blade didn't give his cousins a second thought, and Jessica considered them ineffectual clods.

Her opinion changed when Blade received a phone call from his aunt. They were sitting together on the couch in the den listening to soft music on the stereo.

"Who the devil is that?" Blade scowled at the intrusion.

"The best way to find out is to answer it." Jessica smiled fondly at his impatience.

His displeasure deepened as he said, "Sylvia, this is a surprise."

"You're very hard to reach. I left several messages," she said.

"Really? I didn't get them," he answered blandly.

Jessica shook her head reprovingly, knowing he had. Blade's comments had been very pungent when she suggested he return the calls.

"You should find out why someone is failing to deliver your messages. It's either sloppiness, or something more serious," Sylvia warned direly.

"Like what?"

"Someone—I don't like to make accusations—could be trying to isolate you from your family for personal reasons."

Blade grinned. "Do you suspect Mrs. Bartlett? She did make my favorite lemon cream pie tonight. Do you think she has the hots for me?"

"Joke if you like, but a man in your position has to be cautious about becoming too friendly with the help."

"You don't really think I'm fooling around with Mrs. B.?" he exclaimed incredulously.

"Oh, Blade, don't be so dense! She's not the only female employee in the house."

His eyes glinted dangerously. "If you're referring to Jessica, I don't consider her 'help'."

"Perhaps that was a poor choice of words, but you must admit she hasn't had your advantages."

"How do you know?"

"Well, I...I just assumed. Why else would she be working as a secretary?"

"Larry is a salesman, and Nina's a shop clerk. Are their jobs any more prestigious?"

"How can you...that's utterly...you're completely distorting the facts." Sylvia was sputtering with indignation.

"I don't see it that way, but we won't argue about it. Did you want something special?"

"Just to see how you're getting along." She swallowed her anger like a bitter pill.

"Kevin and I are fine," Blade answered pointedly.

"Oh yes, how is the dear child?"

"Doing well, now. Jessica has done wonders with the boy." He sent her a loving look.

"Do you think it's a good idea to let her get that close to him?"

"Neither of them is contagious," Blade said mockingly.

"Your levity is making this very difficult for me. Your uncle and I are concerned about you, Blade."

"I thought we were talking about Kevin."

"Him, too, of course. But you're the one who's vulnerable. I'd feel a lot happier if that woman were out of the house."

"I'm sure you would, Aunt Sylvia." Blade's eyes danced with laughter. "But may I remind you that my father wanted her here."

"I still say Winston was deranged when he drew up that dreadful will."

"Grant Sutherland is prepared to swear he wasn't."

"Naturally. He made a lot of money out of your father."

"It's futile to argue about it now." Blade was becoming impatient.

Sylvia sensed she was losing him. "I'll leave you with a word of advice. Don't be too trusting. Women who have never had money will do almost anything to get it."

"That holds true for both sexes, including people who already have money. Good night, Sylvia."

Jessica had grown very still as she listened to Blade's side of the conversation. She didn't have to hear Sylvia's part to know the woman was warning him against her.

Blade seemed unaffected. He returned to the couch and settled her back in his arms. "Where were we? I believe I was doing this." He nibbled gently on her ear.

Jessica drew away. "Your aunt accused me of being a fortune hunter, didn't she?"

"I believe the old-fashioned term was adventuress," he teased. "Doesn't that have a saucy ring to it?"

"I'm glad you think it's funny," she said stiffly.

"Of course it's funny. My aunt could be a stand-up comic."

"You weren't always this tolerant of her."

He lifted her chin and gazed at her fondly. "I've mellowed since I met you."

Jessica realized that pursuing the subject would only benefit Sylvia, but she couldn't let it drop. "Do you think I'm only interested in your money, Blade?"

"I know of at least one more thing you're interested in." His tone was playful, but something flickered in his eyes.

With a sinking heart, Jessica felt she'd received her answer.

"Let's go upstairs," he murmured in her ear.

For once she didn't respond to him. "I have a slight headache. I think I'll take an aspirin and go to sleep."

"I'm sorry you're not feeling well," he said gravely.

"It's nothing." She avoided looking at him. "A good night's rest will fix me up."

Jessica went to bed, but not to sleep. She stared at the ceiling, looking for answers to the problem. Sylvia's clumsy warning wasn't necessary. Blade had harbored his own suspicions all along. He would never believe she'd fallen in love with him. They were sexually compatible; that was enough for Blade.

When the year was up he would leave with fond memories. But she would be left with a broken heart. How could she continue their relationship, knowing his opinion of her? Yet how could she not, loving him as she did? It was all the fault of the will. Even if he suddenly asked her to marry him—a remote possibility—would she accept? Blade wasn't the only one who had an aversion to being used.

The door opened quietly, and a slice of light from the hall cast a golden path across the carpet. Blade's silhouette was framed in the doorway.

Jessica sat up. "Is something wrong?"

"I just wanted to see if you felt all right." He came over and stood by the bed.

"Oh . . . yes, my headache is better."

"Why aren't you asleep?"

"I was. You woke me," she lied.

"You couldn't sleep, and neither could I. Are you still angry with me, Jessica?"

"What gave you that idea?" she hedged.

"Credit me with knowing that much about you." She couldn't see his face in the darkness, but his voice was dry.

"That's not much," she answered bitterly.

He sat on the edge of the bed and took both her hands in his. "If I'd known you'd take Sylvia's phone call seriously, I wouldn't have made a joke of it."

"She called specifically to make trouble between us."

"I know. Are you going to let her?"

"Do you expect me to simply laugh off her character assassination?"

"I would think you'd consider the source. Sylvia is a shallow, grasping woman who would do or say anything to accomplish her goals. She's too stupid even to be subtle about it. If I seemed to make light of her call, it was only because I assumed you would, too.''

"You could have said you didn't believe her," Jessica answered uncertainly, trying in vain to read his expression in the dim light.

"That would have dignified her charges." His hands tightened. "Dear heart, don't you know how I feel about you? My whole world falls apart when you shut me out."

In spite of the feeling that nothing had been settled between them, Jessica was powerless to resist when Blade took her in his arms. His avid mouth and fervent caresses succeeded in driving everything else out of her mind.

Blade's relatives were not encouraged after Sylvia's phone call. They had all gathered in the Kilpatrick's plush condominium to listen in.

Sylvia's face was flushed when she hung up. "I can't believe the disrespect I just heard! The way he talked to me, his own aunt, is a positive disgrace. I don't know what's happening in the world. Young people today have absolutely no manners!"

"Not that same old lecture again," Larry said disgustedly. "Give it a rest."

"Don't talk to your mother that way." Carter frowned.

"Stop it, all of you," Nina ordered. "I want to hear what Blade had to say. I gather he resented your call— that's to be expected—but how badly did he react when you bad-mouthed Jessica?"

"I certainly wouldn't put it that way," Sylvia protested. "I was simply pointing out the dangers to a man in Blade's position of becoming involved with designing women."

Nina snorted in an unladylike fashion that deepened her mother's disapproval. "Knowing his track record with the female sex, that's like warning the wolf to watch out for little Red Riding Hood."

Larry looked at her suspiciously. "You're certainly dragging your feet. Did Jessica promise you a piece of the action to switch to her team?"

"Don't be a jerk. I'm just being realistic. Blade has always been a prize. He's used to women chasing after him."

"But this time he has a reason to let one catch him."

"That's true," Nina admitted. "And Jessica has everything going for her. Besides being sexy, she's shrewd."

"Her kind always is," Sylvia sniffed. "Although they're forced to settle for whatever they can get. Men don't marry the women they...ah..."

"Mother, you're priceless." Nina gazed at her with amusement as the older woman came to a delicate halt. "Do you honestly believe that?"

"I most certainly do! And I would hope *you* live by the same high principles you've been taught. No man will respect you if you don't respect yourself."

"Will you save the sermon?" Larry asked irritably. "We're talking money, not morals. The question now is what to do next. Maybe Pop should take Blade out to lunch and talk to him, man to man."

Carter looked dubious. "I doubt if that would be effective. Blade and I have never been close, I regret to say."

"Don't blame yourself," Sylvia advised. "I don't know of anyone he does care about except perhaps that child, Kevin."

"That's it!" Larry exclaimed. "That's the answer. We've been going about this thing all wrong. We should have been sucking up to the kid."

"Must you be so vulgar?" his mother asked with distaste.

His enthusiasm wasn't dampened. "Blade is really gung ho about this parenting thing. He's miffed at us because he thinks we've been neglecting the little brat. If we suddenly see the error of our ways and start killing the kid with kindness, we automatically become the good guys. Blade would be a lot more receptive to well-meant advice."

"After the way we messed things up the last time, Jessica wouldn't let us in the same room with Kevin," Nina remarked.

"She has no authority to keep you away," Sylvia said indignantly. "The boy is your little cousin."

"Blade has given her the authority," Nina replied. "Jessica is running the show over there."

"Then it's time to move to a new theater. How do you feel about a nice intimate family dinner?" Larry asked his mother.

"I think it's an excellent idea," she replied.

"The trick will be to get Blade and Kevin here without Jessica," Nina mused.

"She can scarcely come if she isn't invited," Sylvia said dismissively.

"What if Blade takes it for granted that she *is* invited?"

"Leave that to me. I'll make it quite clear we're having a family get-together, and she doesn't qualify."

"Not yet, anyway," Nina said ironically.

Blade balked at the prospect even before he knew Jessica wasn't included. "It's very thoughtful of you, Sylvia, but I'm afraid we'll have to decline. Wednesday is a school night for Kevin.''

"You can go home early," she assured him.

"He usually has a lot of homework to do after dinner," Blade temporized.

"He can do it after school instead," Sylvia answered implacably.

"I'll have to check with Jessica. She might have other plans."

"That's no problem. I hope you understand this isn't meant as a slight against Jessica, but I'd planned a family evening."

Blade's mouth firmed. "The three of us consider ourselves a family. Jessica has done more for Kevin than a blood relation could have."

"I deserve that criticism," Sylvia said penitently. "My children and I have been terribly remiss, but not intentionally so. People get caught up in their own lives without realizing they're being thoughtless. Haven't you ever neglected someone without meaning to?"

Her words struck a nerve as Blade remembered his earlier preoccupation. "Unfortunately I have," he answered in a muted voice.

"Then surely you'll give us another chance. We really want to become closer to the boy."

"Why does that mean excluding Jessica?"

"Be reasonable, Blade. In spite of my reservations about her, I have nothing but admiration for Jessica's dedication to Kevin. But from what I've heard, he ignores everyone else when she's around. How can we establish a relationship with him under the circumstances?"

"Kevin's devotion to Jessica is understandable," he answered austerely.

"I realize that, but it isn't healthy for him to be completely dependent on one person, especially someone who has no real ties to him. What will happen to him emotionally when Jessica leaves?"

"She won't," he said curtly.

"Not before the year is up perhaps, but what about after that? Kevin needs the security of a family, and we want to give it to him, albeit belatedly. Please don't deny us that privilege, Blade."

"I'm not trying to keep him away from you," he answered slowly. What Sylvia said made sense, if she was sincere.

"Then bring Kevin to dinner on Wednesday night." When he continued to hesitate she said, "We haven't been very close in the past, but this is a chance for all of us to make a fresh start. We owe that to Steven's child."

"I suppose you're right," Blade said heavily.

He stared at the phone for a long time after replacing the receiver, conflict clouding his face. "How am I going to explain it to her?" he muttered.

Jessica was concerned over his brooding expression when she came into the den a few moments later. "Is something wrong, Blade?"

He forced a smile. "No. Everything's dandy."

She would have questioned him further, but Mrs. Bartlett rang the dinner bell.

Blade's behavior at the table appeared perfectly normal. He joked with Kevin and complimented the housekeeper on a favorite dish she'd made for him. But a certain preoccupation told Jessica something was on Blade's mind. She didn't find out what it was until they were almost finished with dinner.

After scooping up the last of his ice cream Kevin asked, "May I be excused? I have a whole bunch of homework to do."

"We'll be up to say good-night later on," Jessica said fondly.

As the youngster prepared to leave Blade said, "Tomorrow I'd like you to do your homework in the afternoon."

"Johnny Ridell's coming home with me after school," Kevin protested. "We're going to build a fort on the beach."

"You'll have to put it off until Thursday."

"Why? I always do my homework at night."

"You won't have time tomorrow. We're going out to dinner." Blade avoided looking at Jessica.

"Oh, boy! That's different." Kevin gazed at his uncle in happy anticipation. "Where are we going?"

"To your Aunt Sylvia's."

Kevin's eagerness fled. "I don't want to."

"That's not very polite. She's your aunt, and she wants to see you."

"I don't care. I don't like her." The youngster looked appealingly at Jessica. "Do I have to go?"

Blade frowned. "It's not up to Jessica. We were invited, and we're going."

"Why do I have to?" Kevin asked mutinously.

"Because they're your relatives, and you barely know them. That isn't right. Friends are important, but family is too. You should get to know yours better."

Jessica sat still as a statue torn between outrage and apprehension. Sylvia was clearly using Kevin as a wedge between Blade and herself. The woman couldn't care less about the child. Why was Blade allowing himself to be deceived?

He was dismissing his nephew's arguments with dwindling patience. Finally Kevin left the room with a reproachful look at Jessica. After he was gone, a pulsing silence fell.

Blade broke it when it became evident that Jessica wasn't going to. "I suppose you disapprove."

"As you pointed out, it isn't up to me," she answered coolly.

"I didn't mean that the way it sounded."

"I think you did. It wasn't difficult for Sylvia to convince you, was it?" she asked bitterly.

"This has nothing to do with you and me." His tone was placating. "What I told Kevin was the truth. Family *is* important. I can't guarantee I'll always be here for him, and you can't be expected to."

Any hope Jessica might have had for a permanent relationship curled up and died. She tried to mask her pain out of pride, but also concern for Kevin.

"What you say is true. But do you honestly think Sylvia and her clan give a damn about Kevin?"

"Not really," he admitted. "But I have to give them the benefit of the doubt for his sake."

"Well, I hope you'll run interference for him because I'm not going to waste an evening with those phonies." When Blade's eyes shifted uncomfortably, Jessica exclaimed, "I'm not invited, am I?"

"You're the lucky one," he mumbled.

Her eyes glittered with anger. "Kevin is just a pawn in this game. You're the one they want to work on. Maybe if you admit the error of your ways and promise not to have anything more to do with me, neither of you will have to suffer through a boring dinner."

"Don't talk like that. You must know how much you mean to me. How can I convince you that I'm only doing this for Kevin?"

"Why bother? I hope you have a delightful evening." She rose to her feet.

"I didn't realize you'd take it this personally." Blade sighed. "I'll call Sylvia and break the date."

"Not on my account. I wouldn't dream of interfering with a family reunion. Just see that his loving relatives don't upset Kevin too much." Jessica left the room with her chin held high.

Anger sustained her for a time, but it couldn't compensate for the desolation that chilled her heart. This was really the end. If Blade cared about her, he wouldn't have let himself be manipulated. And if sex was all that was involved between them, it wasn't enough.

She locked her bedroom door that night.

Jessica was miserable the next day, but her resolve didn't weaken any more than it had the night before when Blade tapped softly at her door. She'd turned on her stomach and put the pillow over her head, even though every fiber of her being cried out for him.

Blade's only acknowledgement of the locked door had been an unaccustomed formality in his manner toward her that morning. He no longer tried to make excuses.

As the afternoon wore on Jessica became more restless and resentful. Finally she went to the phone and dialed her former roommate at work.

"It's good to hear from you," Harriet said after they'd exchanged greetings. "What's doing in the world of the rich and famous?"

"I wouldn't know. I'm just part of the hired help around here." Jessica tried to make it sound like a joke.

"I wouldn't mind having your working conditions."

"Who was it who said, be careful what you wish for. You might get it."

"Is something wrong, Jess?" Harriet asked uncertainly.

"Heavens, no!" Jessica regretted her momentary self-indulgence. "Things couldn't be better, except I miss our old rap sessions. How about having dinner tonight?"

"I can't. I'm going to my brother's engagement party. You remember Brian. He's marrying a darling girl."

"I'm so happy for him. Give him my love."

"Why don't you come to the party with me? It's out your way. I'll pick you up."

"I couldn't do that," Jessica protested.

"Brian will be delighted," Harriet assured her. "It's going to be a mob scene anyway. You'll know half the people there."

Jessica allowed herself to be persuaded because she didn't want to sit home alone, or go to a movie by herself. Just the prospect of being with old friends revived her drooping spirits.

She managed to match Blade's coolness when he said goodbye that evening, but Kevin's unhappiness penetrated her shell of indifference.

"Can't you come with us?" he asked dolefully.

Blade answered before she could, not trying to mask his irritation. "I don't know why you're making such a big deal about a simple dinner."

Restraining herself with an effort, Jessica told Kevin, "Sometimes when you least expect it, you have the best time."

His dejected face tugged at her heartstrings, but when Harriet picked her up a little later, Jessica resolved to put

Kevin out of her mind. As Blade had so charmingly pointed out, she wasn't part of his inner circle.

For a time she did forget about both Dunsmuirs. As Harriet had predicted, she knew a lot of people at the party and was welcomed with enthusiasm. Especially by old boyfriends and would-be new ones.

It was a gala evening, with many toasts to the prospective bride and groom. Jessica, who usually drank very little, joined in every one.

"I'd take it easy if I were you," Harriet remarked. "How many glasses of champagne have you had?"

Jessica giggled. "I don't know. Arithmetic was never my best subject."

"Oh, brother! It's a good thing I'm driving you home."

"Not necessarily. Several very gallant men have offered me a ride."

"To your house or theirs?" Harriet asked bluntly.

"Don't be a nag."

"What's gotten into you, Jessica? You've always been smarter than that about men."

"Sure. Nobody takes advantage of Jessica Lawrence. I can tell when a man wants only one thing from me." She lifted her glass in a sardonic salute. "It just takes a little while to sink in."

As Harriet looked after her with a worried frown Jessica was twirled onto the makeshift dance floor in the arms of an eager partner, who had been waiting his turn.

In spite of her friend's worries Jessica refused all other offers and went home with Harriet when the evening was over.

"I'm glad you got sensible," Harriet remarked while they were driving.

"That's the story of my life, except for a couple of notable exceptions." The champagne glow was wearing off. Jessica leaned her head back and closed her eyes.

"I can tell something's bothering you. Would you like to talk about it?" Harriet asked quietly.

"It wouldn't do any good. Mine is the age-old story. I fell in love with the wrong man."

"Blade?"

Jessica nodded. "You'd think I'd know better, wouldn't you?"

"I guess it was to be expected, living together and all. He's a very glamorous man. But you're not exactly a plain Jane, yourself. I can't believe he isn't affected by the same set of circumstances."

Jessica gave a harsh laugh. "I thought we were talking about love."

"Oh." Comprehension dawned on Harriet's face.

"Well, live and learn." Jessica changed the subject. "Tonight was fun. Let's get together again next week."

She tried to close the car door softly when Harriet pulled up in front of the house, but the sound was like a pistol shot in the quiet neighborhood. The two women lowered their voices as they made plans to phone each other soon.

Jessica was tired but not sleepy. Instead of going to her room she wandered into the den. The room was lit by moonlight streaming through the windows facing the beach.

She stared out at a scene of majestic beauty. The restless ocean was frilled with phosphorescent wavelets, miniature versions of the more powerful waves that dashed themselves against the shore in a compulsive attempt at self-destruction.

Like me, Jessica thought somberly. That was the course she was on. Knowing as much, she realized the sensible thing to do was cut her losses and make a new start. Several men at the party had asked to see her again, but she'd put them off with vague excuses. Why? What was the point in mourning the loss of a relationship that had existed only in her own mind?

Jessica was so engrossed in her somber thoughts that she didn't hear Blade enter the room. His sudden reflection in the glass frightened her.

"Oh, it's you!" she gasped. "You startled me."

"I'm sorry. I heard you come home, but you didn't come upstairs. I came down to see if you were all right."

"I'm fine." She turned back to the window. "You can go back to sleep."

"I wasn't asleep," he said quietly.

"You should be. It's late."

The tiny sensors on her skin were tinglingly aware of him. Even in the dim light she'd glimpsed the expanse of bare chest revealed by his carelessly tied navy silk robe. Prior knowledge supplied details about the rest of his lithe body.

"Where were you tonight?" he asked.

"I went to a party."

"You didn't mention it earlier."

"I didn't think it was necessary to account for my free time."

"I wasn't implying that you did," he answered patiently. "I was simply surprised when you weren't here when we got home."

"I don't doubt it. I've been boringly predictable, but that's going to change."

"You could never be boring." His voice was husky.

Jessica refused to let it affect her. "Fortunately I met some men tonight who agree with you. They made me realize what I've been missing."

Blade's expression was inscrutable in the dim light. "I wasn't aware that you felt unfulfilled."

"You never thought about it as long as your own needs were met," she lashed out.

His eyes narrowed. "Are you saying yours weren't?"

Jessica refused to think about the rapturous nights in his arms. "I'd rather not talk about it. I'm going to bed."

As she started to brush by him, Blade's fingers closed around her wrist. "Not until you answer my question."

"I don't want to argue with you." She tried to pull away, but his hand was like a steel band.

"There won't be any argument. Just tell me I put my own gratification before yours all those nights. Tell me what way I failed to satisfy you."

"Adequate sex doesn't make up for everything," she said stubbornly.

"Adequate!" he exclaimed incredulously. "Is that the way you'd describe our lovemaking? I certainly must have failed you if that's your recollection. You'll have to share some of the blame, however, because you put on one hell of an act."

Jessica's cheeks warmed, remembering her own cries of joy as Blade had brought her to the peak of sensation. "All you care about is your prowess as a lover," she said angrily. "Any other feelings I might have are unimportant."

"You don't really believe that."

"You've made it abundantly clear," she answered tightly.

"I'd be devastated if I didn't know what's really troubling you. You're angry about tonight, and I don't blame you," he said slowly. "I'm angry, too—at myself. I honestly thought Sylvia had a conscience somewhere in her selfish soul. I hoped that she wanted to open her heart to Kevin, to give him some of the love his parents would have if they'd lived."

Jessica was diverted for the moment. "What happened to change your mind?"

Blade made a sound of disgust. "When we first got there they were all over the poor kid. Elvis Presley would have been turned off by the attention."

"They don't know much about ten-year-olds." She tried to be fair.

"And they care less. After they'd put on a big display for my benefit, they ignored him completely. As you correctly surmised, I was their target. With varying degrees of subtlety I was warned against marriage, engagements and long-term relationships. They stopped just short of suggesting I become a monk, probably out of fear I'd take the vows of poverty literally and donate my money to the church."

"Were the warnings general, or did my name come up?"

"You were covered under a blanket indictment of all females."

"I can't believe I didn't come in for special mention."

He smiled wryly. "Sylvia did remark that you were a very clever woman. She didn't make it sound like a compliment."

"It takes one to know one," Jessica said disdainfully.

"She's more devious than I gave her credit for," he agreed. "But that's no excuse for my behavior. Can you forgive me?"

"It isn't that simple. Perhaps I can understand that you went there for Kevin's sake, but not the way you resent my affection for him."

"I'm *grateful* for that!"

"When it suits your purpose. You made it quite clear tonight that my advice concerning him wasn't welcome."

"I didn't mean to give that impression. I was irritated with Sylvia for excluding you, and frustrated because I felt I had to go along with her. Then when Kevin gave me a hard time I snapped at him thoughtlessly, hurting both of you. I tried to make it up to him. Will you let me make it up to you?"

"I don't know, Blade." She sighed. "Maybe this whole thing between us has been a mistake."

"You can't forgive me?" he asked gravely.

"It isn't that. I can see how everything happened, but our casual affair is getting complicated by too many things."

"I never thought of our relationship as a casual affair."

"What else would you call it? We're together because we have to be. When the year is up we'll go our separate ways."

"No one can predict the future. The present is what counts." He reached out and touched her cheek gently. "I care deeply about you, Jessica. Not just your beautiful body. I care about you as a person."

"I wish I could believe that," she murmured, gazing at him searchingly.

His hand dropped to his side. "I could try to convince you, but I won't. You'll have to make up your own mind."

Did that mean he didn't care? Couldn't he tell she wanted him to take her in his arms and kiss away all her doubts? But Blade's expressionless face gave no clue to his real feelings.

After an indecisive moment Jessica said, "I'll think about it." She moved toward the door. "I'm going to bed."

He watched her go but didn't follow her.

She got undressed and put on her nightgown, listening for Blade's footsteps without knowing what she'd do if he came to her room. He didn't even come upstairs until a long while later, and then he went to his own bedroom.

Jessica stared into the darkness, torturing herself with memories of happier nights when Blade had come to her eagerly, impatient at having to wait. They'd satisfied their passion in infinite ways, but they'd also talked for hours about every conceivable topic. They didn't always agree, which led to lively discussion.

That wasn't the behavior of a man who was only interested in sex. If Blade was truthful about respecting her as a person, then she was the world's prize idiot. Sylvia would be delighted to know how effective she'd been at causing trouble between them.

Jessica got out of bed and reached for her robe, then thought better of it. She walked across the hall in her bare feet and quietly opened Blade's door without knocking. Anticipation rippled up her spine as she pictured how she'd wake him.

Blade wasn't asleep. He sat up in bed and looked at her with luminous eyes. "Does this mean you've made up your mind?"

She sat down on the side of the bed. "I told you I'd think about it."

His torso was rigid with the effort not to touch her. "What did you decide?"

One lace-trimmed strap slid down her arm as she casually moved her shoulder. "I was really impressed that you admired my mind," she said artlessly.

"That doesn't preclude appreciating your body, also." His voice was hoarse as he stared at her breast. It was almost fully exposed as the nightgown strap slipped lower.

She smiled alluringly. "You showed such restraint that I wasn't sure."

He reached for her and yanked both straps down, pulling the gown to her waist. "You've just destroyed the last shred of it."

Clasping her tightly in his arms his mouth devoured hers with pent-up longing. Jessica's hunger was as great as his. She moved against him with such urgency that they toppled together onto the bed, their limbs entwined.

Blade disposed of their encumbering nightclothes without releasing Jessica or relinquishing her mouth. He murmured broken words of desire against her lips as he caressed her feverishly.

Their passion flared brightly before subsiding into a muted glow that bathed them in warmth. Jessica remained sheltered in Blade's arms, too contented to move.

"I don't know what I'd do without you," he murmured some time later, tightening his grip.

"You're about to find out." She stirred reluctantly. "If I stay here any longer we'll both fall asleep."

"Stay with me tonight," he urged.

"I can't." She slipped out of bed before her resolve failed. When he got up, too, and lifted her into his arms she said, "Please, Blade. We might oversleep, and Kevin gets up early."

"I know. I'm just taking you back to your room."

In her darkened bedroom Blade placed Jessica tenderly under the covers. But after bending to kiss her good-night, he slid into bed next to her.

"You can't stay." Her protest was faint because Blade's taut body made it difficult to refuse him. "We agreed."

"I'll go back to my room before morning."

"It's almost morning now. You won't get any sleep."

He chuckled softly and whispered arousing words in her ear. As his hand trailed erotically over her body, time ceased to have any meaning.

Chapter Ten

Jessica and Blade were blissfully happy after that night, immune to outside influences. Not that they weren't present.

Sylvia demonstrated her thick hide by calling often in the days that followed, inundating Blade with invitations. He refused all of them curtly.

Jessica stayed strictly out of it, knowing Blade could take care of himself. But when Sylvia turned her attention to Kevin, making the boy miserable, Jessica felt it was time to act.

She had a sharp exchange with her over the phone after Sylvia tried to pressure Kevin into going to a birthday party for the grandson of one of her friends. Jessica took the phone after Kevin sent her a silent, agonized cry for help.

"What seems to be the problem, Sylvia?" she asked evenly.

"Nothing that concerns you," the other woman answered coldly. "Put my nephew back on the line."

"He's gone outside to play."

"How dare you interfere between us?" Sylvia bristled.

"I gathered your business together was concluded."

"You saw to that! I'm sure you also told Kevin to refuse my invitation."

"No, that was his own idea."

"Do you expect me to believe that? All children enjoy birthday parties."

"Where they don't know a soul?"

"These are lovely children from the best families," Sylvia informed her. "Kevin should get to know them."

"He's a little young for networking," Jessica remarked dryly.

"What gives you the right to decide what's good for him? If Blade weren't completely besotted by you he'd see the kind of scheming woman you are."

"You've certainly told him often enough," Jessica answered ironically.

"Don't crow too soon. You haven't won yet." Sylvia's voice was shrill. "Blade is just amusing himself with you. Don't think he'll marry you, because he won't."

Jessica hung up without replying. She tried not to let Sylvia's crude attack bother her, in spite of the fact that her prophecy was probably accurate. The woman's maneuvering had to be stopped because of Kevin.

Jessica considered the possible ways. She didn't like to go to Blade. He would overreact, which wouldn't accomplish anything. Carter was a cipher, without the will to stand up to his stronger wife, and Larry would have to study before he could qualify as an idiot. That left only Nina. Jessica dialed her number without enthusiasm.

She was direct when Nina came to the phone. "This is Jessica. I want you to meet me for lunch tomorrow."

"Why?" Nina asked with equal bluntness. "You've never made any secret of how you feel about me."

"Just be at the Oasis at one o'clock. And come alone."

Jessica hung up without waiting for a reply. She was fairly certain Nina would show up. Curiosity would bring her if nothing else.

Jessica's surmise was correct. Nina was already at the restaurant drinking a martini when Jessica arrived.

"I was expecting dark glasses and a trench coat," she drawled, eyeing Jessica's trim beige suit and high-heeled pumps. "You sounded so cloak-and-dagger on the phone."

"You've always misjudged me." Jessica took the chair opposite hers.

"My family perhaps, but not I." Nina's gaze turned to Jessica's shining hair and long-lashed green eyes. "I always knew you were a formidable opponent."

"I want to talk to you about your family."

"You don't waste time in chitchat, do you?" Nina asked sardonically.

"What's the point in pretending this is a social get-together? I know you're curious about why I asked you here."

"And you want to spend as little time with me as possible."

"I'm sure the feeling is mutual," Jessica answered evenly.

"I've never cared a lot about women like you," Nina admitted.

Jessica's eyes started to smolder. "Spare me a critique of my morals."

"Good God, I couldn't care less. I meant I don't appreciate being with gorgeous sexpots who make me look even uglier than usual."

Jessica stared at her in amazement. Nina couldn't be called pretty, but she had an interesting face. Almond-shaped, dark eyes were her most striking feature. Slightly tilted above high cheekbones, they gave her face an exotic flavor. Her figure was good, and she dressed flamboyantly but in excellent taste.

She was defiantly defensive under Jessica's scrutiny. "Don't bother saying something polite. I know what I look like."

"I wonder if you do," Jessica said slowly.

"My mother's told me since I was a child. 'Isn't it a shame you don't have Larry's blond curls?'" she mimicked mockingly. "'Why couldn't you have inherited my nose instead of your father's?'"

"She said those things to you?" Jessica asked incredulously.

Nina shrugged. "I could see them myself in the mirror. Luckily I didn't wind up with Larry's brain. That would really be adding insult to injury."

Jessica agreed privately, but she was appalled at the insight she was gaining. Through massive insensitivity Sylvia had made her daughter insecure. Nina compensated with an acid tongue and an air of indifference, yet underneath her caustic manner she felt inadequate.

"I suppose I shouldn't be so hard on Larry. I get impatient with him because I see all of my own rotten qualities reflected," Nina said in a burst of honesty.

"You're nothing like your brother," Jessica protested.

"That's the first nice thing you ever said to me." Nina laughed. "But you're wrong. We're both leeches. Neither of us ever did a thing on our own in our lives."

"Why not?"

"Partly through laziness, but mostly because we have rich parents and no talent."

"Your first two reasons might be valid, but the last one is a cop-out. Everyone has talent in one area or another. Or at least aptitude."

"You're looking at the exception to the rule," Nina said wryly.

"I don't believe that. You must be interested in something."

"Ah, that's a different matter. Being interested and being able to do something about it aren't the same thing."

"What would you do if you could?" Jessica asked curiously.

"Marry a rich man so Mother would get off my back."

"I asked what *you* would like to do."

"You sound like a frustrated psychiatrist. Okay, Doc, the only thing I've shown any talent for is flower arranging. I took a couple of courses and I was good at it. Isn't that a hoot?"

Jessica was careful to conceal her surprise. "I'm impressed. My attempts are so bad you can tell they were done by an amateur with two left thumbs."

"Most people have the same problem. You need to start with the right equipment like florist's foam and plastic covered wire. But that's only the beginning. Varying the length of the stems is important for an interesting arrangement." Nina's cynical expression changed to animation as she talked about a subject that obviously intrigued her. She stopped suddenly, her face filled with self-mockery. "How's that for a useless talent?"

"Why are you putting yourself down? Not everyone can do what you do."

"Big deal. There's no money in it."

"Is that the only thing that matters to you?"

Jessica's unconcealed disdain penetrated Nina's mask of bored detachment. "Nothing boils me more than condescension from women like you who have everything," she said angrily.

"You're joking!" Jessica stared at her uncomprehendingly. "You think I'm privileged? I work for a living. Until Mr. Dunsmuir died I shared a small apartment with a roommate to save expenses. You work when and if you feel like it, because your parents will always get you another job if you become bored with your present one. What could I possibly have that you don't have?"

"Self-respect and a purpose in life," Nina answered quietly.

This was a side of the other woman that Jessica hadn't guessed at. She hesitated for a moment before saying tentatively, "If you really feel that way, why don't you do something about it?"

"Like what?" Lines of discontent were etched on Nina's face. "Why do you think I want a share of the money Uncle Winston left? For once in my life I wouldn't have to run to my parents for every extra nickel."

"You'd still be taking handouts, simply from a different source. That money might make you independent for a while, but it wouldn't change the life you're so dissatisfied with."

"What do you suggest I do? In case you've forgotten, I'm not trained for anything." Nina smiled derisively.

"Maybe I could make up flower arrangements and peddle them door-to-door."

Jessica gazed at her thoughtfully as the germ of an idea took hold. "Have you ever helped your mother with the flowers when she gives parties?"

"No. She always orders something elaborate from a florist. All her friends do." Nina shot her a quick look. "If you're suggesting I start a little cottage industry among my mother's acquaintances, forget it."

"That wasn't what I had in mind. You need to stop relying on your mother and start concentrating on your own efforts."

"At what? I don't see what you're driving at."

"Parties are a way of life in your social circles," Jessica explained patiently. "Private parties, charity affairs, dances at the country club. All of those events use floral pieces for decoration—hundreds, sometimes thousands of dollars' worth. Somebody arranges all those flowers. Why not you?"

"I'm not a professional," Nina protested.

"You will be as soon as someone pays you to do it."

"But I wouldn't know where to start. Why would anyone hire me?"

"Because you're good," Jessica answered crisply. "You told me so yourself."

"I *am* good! But who would believe it? Where would I get customers? I'm not going to ask for charity from my friends. That would be the ultimate humiliation."

"Forget about your friends. I'm talking about a valid service." Jessica considered the matter. "One possibility would be to hook up with a caterer. When I used to arrange parties for Mr. Dunsmuir, the caterer also provided the flowers, but I'm sure he contracted out for them. Why not ask around at various catering firms? You must know a lot of them.''

"Dozens." Nina looked slightly dazed. "Do you think one of them would really give me a chance?''

"What do you have to lose? Ask them.''

"I will! Oh, Jessica, do you know what this might lead to? I could build my own business and do something I enjoy. How can I ever thank you?''

"You can do me a favor,'' Jessica answered quietly.

"Anything! Just name it.''

Jessica hesitated. "What I'm about to ask might seem like a conflict of interests.''

"It's about you and Blade, isn't it? You want me to get my family off your back.''

"I don't care what they do to *me*. I want them to leave Kevin alone.''

Nina looked surprised. "There's no way they could tap into his money.''

"This has nothing to do with money," Jessica said impatiently. "Kevin was a very insecure little boy when he first came here. He was fighting the whole world. Blade and I have worked hard to give him a normal life, and now your mother is undermining us by trying to pry him out of his safe niche. She can continue her efforts to make trouble between Blade and me, just tell her to stop using Kevin to do it.''

"You really care about the boy, don't you? You're not simply putting on an act for Blade's benefit.''

Jessica smiled mockingly. "Don't you credit me with more potent methods of persuasion?''

"I told them they were fighting a losing battle.''

"An unnecessary one," Jessica said tersely. "That's what makes Sylvia's intrigue so annoying. Your inheritance is safe. When the year is up, Blade will go back overseas—still single."

Nina slanted a glance at her. "You don't have to keep my hopes up. I never really counted on the money."

"I'm telling you the simple truth. You can believe it or not."

"I know I haven't acted very intelligently, but I'm not a complete fool, Jessica. Blade is crazy about you. He wouldn't listen to a word against you the other night."

"Your mother isn't exactly subtle," Jessica said dryly.

"No one could ever accuse her of that," Nina agreed. "But Blade's reaction spoke volumes. I've seen him with other girls through the years. Blade and I used to be closer at one time. I can tell you he was never this intense about any woman."

Jessica concentrated on lining up her silverware. "That's gratifying, but it doesn't change anything."

"Are you saying you don't love him?"

Jessica selected her words carefully. "Blade and I have a good relationship. We enjoy each other's company, and we both care for Kevin."

"That's not what I asked you."

"My feelings have nothing to do with it," Jessica said with finality. "Just tell your mother and brother to back off. I haven't fought back so far, but I will for Kevin's sake."

Blade disapproved of Jessica's luncheon with his cousin. "Why would you waste time with her?" he asked disgustedly.

"You're too hard on Nina. That brittle manner of hers is just an act."

"I'll admit she's the best of the lot, but that's not say- ing much."

"She told me you two used to be friends."

"Nina was at our house a lot. Sometimes I think she was closer to *my* mother than she was to her own."

"Who could blame her?" Jessica asked scornfully.

"She didn't have an ideal childhood," he admitted. "Nina wasn't a bad kid. Too bad she turned into such a terrible adult. At least she's finally decided to start working seriously instead of simply waiting around for her inheritance."

The implication was that she was going to get it. Jessica knew that, but it hurt anyway. Blade didn't have to underscore the fact that he had no intention of marrying.

"Maybe she realized money won't solve her problem." Jessica sighed.

"No, it's been known to create more problems." His face was somber. Once again the terms of the will loomed between them like a concrete barrier.

Except for moments like that when reality intruded on their idyll, Jessica and Blade were blissfully happy. Nina had evidently delivered her warning, and Sylvia decided to be prudent. The days rolled by without a serious cloud on the horizon.

Nina's life was on the upswing, too. She'd joined a small catering firm run by a man named Riley O'Rourke, and was scheduled to do her first big party.

"It couldn't have turned out better," she reported to Jessica the day after. "We were a great team. The tables looked beautiful, and Riley did a fabulous job. I never tasted better hors d'oeuvres."

"Did he try them out on you before the party?"

"No, I sort of stayed around to help. Riley's just getting started and he needed an extra pair of hands. I helped serve."

"Does your mother know about this?" Jessica asked incredulously.

"She'd have a fit, wouldn't she?" Nina laughed. "But I enjoyed myself. I intend to learn everything I can about the catering business."

"I didn't know you were interested in cooking."

"I'm not. I meant the business end of it. I've developed an unexpected aptitude for bookkeeping. Riley's hopeless at keeping track of expenses, so I offered to do it."

His name cropped up constantly in Nina's frequent calls. She described what a struggle it was to get started but expressed implicit faith in Riley. Jessica became curious to meet the man. She came up with an idea that would accomplish two purposes.

The next time Nina called Jessica remarked casually, "I've been thinking about having a small cocktail buffet. Would Riley be interested in catering it? I'd want you to do the flowers, naturally."

"No way," Nina answered promptly. "You said yourself I should forget about favors from friends. Business is a little slow right now because we're a new firm, but word will get around."

"This isn't a favor. I'm offering a straight business proposition. If you don't want the job I'll call another caterer."

"How about Barty?" Nina asked cautiously.

"I can't ask her to do that much extra work."

"You're really sure this isn't a handout?" Nina was still suspicious.

"Don't be ridiculous. I'll expect first-rate quality, and if I don't get it you'll hear from me."

"You'll get it." Nina became enthusiastic once she was convinced. "Riley is the best."

Jessica suggested that Blade invite his friends, too, and the list they collaborated on grew lengthy. The small gathering she'd planned turned into a gala affair.

Late in the afternoon on the Saturday they'd chosen, Jessica walked around the house fluffing sofa cushions and straightening knickknacks with a proprietary air. This house had become home to her. How could she leave it? A sudden rush of melancholy washed over her as she gazed out at the patio.

The thick carpet muffled Blade's footsteps as he entered the room. He put his arms around her and kissed the nape of her neck. "Is this all you have to do, stare off into space? I thought you'd be rushing around getting ready."

She tilted her head onto his shoulder. "Everything's under control."

"In that case, how about coming upstairs with me?" He blew softly in her ear.

"I'm waiting for the caterer."

"You mean I've been replaced by a cook?"

"Temporarily."

"Are you holding out for a better offer?"

"You haven't offered me anything," she answered lightly.

Blade's playful expression became guarded, but before he could answer, Mrs. Bartlett came to say the caterer had arrived.

Jessica hadn't known quite what to expect, but it would never have been someone like Riley O'Rourke. He looked like a man who would be more at home on a football field than in a kitchen. His massive frame and craggy features were intimidating, an impression that was dispelled by a pair of friendly blue eyes and an easy manner.

"This is Riley." Nina introduced the dark-haired giant proudly.

"Nina has told me very good things about you," Jessica said politely.

"She might be a little prejudiced." He smiled. "But I hope you'll be satisfied. I'll start bringing things in."

When he'd gone out to the van Nina asked eagerly, "What do you think?"

"He's a little overwhelming. Are you sure he knows his way around a kitchen?" Jessica was having second thoughts about the success of her party. Nina wasn't exactly a disinterested critic. Even Riley admitted that.

"He's awesome. You'll see."

Nina's judgment was vindicated a short time later when Riley brought in trays of canapés. They were pretty enough to be featured in a gourmet magazine. Precisely cut triangles and rounds of bread were covered with a variety of piquant and colorful foods—pink shrimp, sliced green olives on a bed of cream cheese, smoked oysters surrounded by a fringe of chopped parsley. The variety was endless. When Jessica commented admiringly, Riley offered her a taste.

"They all look so good." She inspected the tray indecisively. "I don't know which one to choose."

"I'll make up a plate for you to take in the other room," Nina said.

"That's a nice way of telling me to get lost." Jessica laughed.

"We have work to do," Nina said frankly.

Riley was alternating his attention between stove and sink, too busy to give her more than an absent smile, so Jessica took her sampling of hors d'oeuvres and left them alone. She made a detour to the bar for a bottle of champagne and two glasses, then carried everything up-stairs.

Blade was padding around his bedroom with only a towel wrapped around his waist. He was barefoot, and the crisp hair on his chest was damp from his recent shower.

When he saw Jessica a broad smile broke out on his handsome face. "I knew you'd come to your senses and dump the cook."

"Don't be so sure of yourself. It was the other way around. He was more interested in his pots and pans than he was in me."

"The man shouldn't be left alone with sharp knives."

"He gave me a consolation prize." She held out the plate. "Don't they look divine?"

"Not bad," Blade said after tasting a canapé. "And champagne, too. What have I done to deserve this?" He twisted off the cork and poured the golden liquid into the two glasses.

"Nothing yet. I want you in my debt."

He took her glass and placed it on the bedside table before taking her in his arms. "I like to pay my debts promptly," he remarked throatily.

"Not now, Blade. They might need me for something."

"I need you more." His hands wandered down her back to cup her buttocks while his lips trailed across her cheek.

"You're confusing necessity with desire." Jessica's laughter had a slight catch in it.

He didn't even bother to deny it. "You're the most desirable woman since Helen of Troy," he murmured.

"Would you fight a war over me?" she asked wistfully.

He chuckled deeply. "I'm a lover, sweetheart, not a fighter."

She moved away abruptly. "Your timing is faulty. Unless you expect to greet our guests in a towel, you'd better get dressed."

"What's wrong, Jessica?" he asked quietly, his playful mood disappearing. "I could tell something was bothering you when I came home. What is it?"

"You're imagining things. I'm just preoccupied with the party. It's always chancy when you mix two groups of people who don't know each other."

Her explanation appeared to satisfy him. "It's going to be a great party," he assured her, selecting a toast point mounded with pâté. "Especially after they taste these things."

"You'll have to meet Riley. In addition to his other talents, he's quite a hunk. I think Nina is in love with him."

"A chef? Sylvia will have screaming hysterics."

"If she finds out," Jessica agreed.

"Keep a good thought. Maybe their affair will run its course before Sylvia catches on."

"I know this will come as a huge surprise to you, but some people form permanent attachments," she said coldly.

"Jessica, wait!" he called as she stalked toward the door, but she kept on going.

The house had been transformed when she got downstairs. Vases holding tall branches of yellow forsythia brightened up dark corners, and various tables held bowls of daffodils and tulips. As a centerpiece on the buffet table, Nina had used a silver and crystal epergne. The many glass bowls on the branching arms were filled with roses of every hue surrounded by delicate sprays of baby's breath. The result was a fragrant, colorful tower of flowers.

"You're a genius!" Jessica exclaimed when the other woman joined her in the dining room. "I never expected anything like this."

"Wait till you get the bill." Nina grinned. "Come see what I've done on the patio."

Brilliant geraniums in small pots were spaced along the length of the low retaining wall, with a hurricane lamp between each pot. The flickering candles cast a soft, yet festive glow in the gathering darkness.

"I love it! This will be perfect for dancing later. Isn't it beautiful, Blade?" Jessica asked, catching sight of him in the doorway.

"Very nice. You have unexpected talent," he said to Nina.

"I figured I'd better develop some instead of counting on my inheritance," she answered, glancing at Jessica.

"I want Blade to meet Riley if he isn't too busy," Jessica said quickly.

"I'm sure he can spare a minute," Nina replied.

"It's nice to meet some of Nina's family," Riley said a few moments later as the two men shook hands.

"Blade is the only one I'd introduce you to," Nina said.

"You can imagine what the rest of them are like if I'm the best of the lot." Blade laughed.

"I've read your news stories," Riley said. "I'd like to talk to you sometime about the situation over there."

"We'll get together," Blade promised.

As the doorbell rang and he and Jessica walked toward the hall together, Blade said, "Nina's taste is improving. He seems like a nice fellow."

After the guests arrived both were kept busy seeing that people met and mingled, but that was their only duty. The actual work of the party was completely taken care of by Riley and Nina.

Jessica couldn't get over a sense of shock when she saw Nina in a black uniform and white apron passing hors d'oeuvres. This was a woman who had always looked down on the working classes. No evidence of that attitude showed as she moved unobtrusively through the guests in a thoroughly professional manner. Her mask slipped only once—when she winked at Jessica.

After the cocktail hour hot dishes were served on the buffet in the dining room. Again Riley distinguished himself with unusual casseroles and platters of perfectly seasoned sliced turkey and rare roast beef.

Afterward people drifted onto the terrace to dance. Music from the stereo in the den was piped through outside speakers.

Jessica and Blade caught only passing glimpses of each other during the evening. Finally he came looking for her.

"I haven't seen you all night. Come and dance with me."

"You're supposed to dance with the guests," she said.

"I've done my duty," he answered firmly.

He led her outside where couples were dancing languorously under a full moon. Jessica moved into Blade's arms with the ease of long familiarity, enjoying, as she always did, the masculine perfection of his body. They danced together silently, without needing words to communicate. Neither was aware of the knowing looks cast their way. When the music stopped they drew apart reluctantly, their eyes meeting in an unspoken promise.

Sometime later, Jessica and Harriet finally found a quiet moment to exchange a few words, but the interval didn't last long. A woman waved from across the room and started toward them.

"Here comes Debbie." Harriet didn't sound pleased. "I was surprised to see her here tonight. You two were never friendly."

"We still aren't," Jessica answered tersely.

She and Debbie had gone to high school together, but they'd never cared for each other. Debbie was a fierce competitor who'd never learned to take defeat gracefully. She'd been especially resentful when Jessica beat her out for a seat on the student council.

"Why did you invite her?" Harriet asked.

"I didn't. She's Jim Ogilvy's date."

"He used to be such a sensible guy," Harriet said as the other woman joined them.

"Wonderful party," Debbie remarked.

"I'm glad you're enjoying it," Jessica answered politely.

"You've done very well for yourself." Debbie glanced around the gracious room.

"This house doesn't belong to me. I only work here." Debbie snickered. "I like your fringe benefits."

"What is that supposed to mean?" Jessica asked ominously.

Debbie gazed at her with exaggerated innocence. "Not many employers would let you use their house to throw a party."

"It's a joint venture. Blade's friends are here, too."

"How democratic of him to mingle with the hired help," Debbie drawled.

"You're way off base," Harriet said angrily. "Jessica holds a very important position here. Blade depends on her for a lot of things."

"Yes, I know. I saw them dancing together."

Jessica fought a losing battle with her rising temper. "I remember now why we were never friends," she said coldly.

"You've got me all wrong, Jessica. I *admire* you for going after the gold ring. You always did say you intended to marry a rich man." Debbie's eyes widened as she looked over Jessica's shoulder. "Oops, I hope I haven't spoiled your game plan."

Jessica turned to find Blade standing behind her, his face impassive. He had to have heard Debbie's malicious remark. She'd made sure of that.

He didn't give any indication. His voice was matter-of-fact as he said, "Nina would like to see you in the kitchen when you have a moment."

"Oh...I...yes, of course."

Jessica knew her stuttering response made her sound guilty of something. She wanted desperately to explain, but she realized the impossibility at that time. With a feeling of hopelessness she excused herself and made her way to the kitchen.

The stove, sink and countertops were spotless. The only evidence that a party had taken place was the large coffee urn, still plugged in.

"We're ready to leave," Nina informed her.

"Okay. I'll write you a check."

"Blade already took care of it, including a big tip." Nina grinned. "I just wanted to say goodbye and thank you."

"I'm the one who should thank you," Jessica said. "You both did a great job."

"Riley's the one who deserves the credit. I only did the menial work."

"She's too modest." He gazed fondly at Nina. "I don't know what I ever did without her. It was nice meeting you, Jessica. I hope to see you again."

"Count on it," she answered.

At least the course of one love affair was running smoothly, Jessica thought. Why did her own relationship with Blade have to swing back and forth like a pendulum? She sighed, then pinned a determined smile on her face and returned to the party.

During the rest of the evening Blade kept his distance. Jessica tried to tell herself that was normal, that he was only doing what she'd told him to do, but all the enjoyment had gone out of the party. She couldn't wait for it to end.

When the last guest had departed Jessica said, "I was beginning to think they'd never leave."

Blade looked at her with a raised eyebrow. "I thought you were enjoying yourself."

"I was, but I want to talk to you. Let's go in the den."

"Can't it wait until morning? I'm all talked out."

"This is important, Blade. I could tell Debbie gave you the wrong impression tonight."

His smile was humorless. "Don't worry about it. We all have friends who are indiscreet."

"She isn't a friend of mine, and she knew exactly what she was doing. Debbie was spiteful as a girl, and she hasn't changed."

Jessica knew by the look on Blade's face that he didn't believe her. Why had she taken that approach? Even to her own ears she sounded defensive.

"If she's that undesirable, you showed remarkable forbearance in inviting her to the party," he remarked.

"I *didn't* invite her! She was here as the date of an old friend of mine. But that's beside the point. The important thing is that what you overheard was misleading."

"You never said your ambition was to marry a rich man?"

"We all said things like that when we were sixteen years old. We also said we were going to become astronauts or movie stars. It was something different every week, some adolescent fantasy. We didn't know what we wanted in those days. Don't you remember how it was?"

"No. The only thing I ever wanted to be was a foreign correspondent."

"You were an unusual teenager."

"Possibly." He walked past her toward the living room. "You can go to bed. I'll turn out the lights down here."

His coolly remote manner made Jessica realize the futility of trying to convince him. Frustration and anger filled her as she climbed the stairs. This was the last time she would ever offer Blade any explanations. He didn't deserve them.

Chapter Eleven

Blade was making breakfast when Jessica came downstairs the next morning. He greeted her pleasantly, without any of the reserve he'd shown the night before.

"You're just in time. How would you like your eggs?" He glanced over inquiringly.

"None for me, thanks. All I want is a cup of coffee."

"Nina left a mountain of food in the refrigerator," he commented.

She took a cup and saucer from the cupboard. "That's good. I hope Kevin won't mind eating leftovers." The youngster had spent the night before at a friend's house.

When they were seated at the kitchen table Blade said tentatively, "Jessica, about last night . . ."

"I think it was quite successful," she said evenly, not allowing him to go on. The time for discussion was past. She picked up the newspaper. "Would you like the front part or the sports section?"

"The front page if you weren't planning to read it," he answered quietly after a look at her set face.

Jessica refused all of Blade's overtures that day and went to bed early. She rather expected him to come to her room after Kevin was asleep, but he didn't. Which was wise of him. She had no intention of letting herself be used by a man who had such a low opinion of her.

The next night after work he came into the den and handed her a square, tissue wrapped box.

"What's this?" she asked suspiciously.

"You told me the other night that I'd never given you anything, and I realized it's true."

"It was a joke! I wasn't hinting."

"I know that, but this is something I'd like you to have."

The tissue wrapping covered a velvet box. Inside, on a bed of white satin was a sparkling sapphire pendant suspended from a fine gold chain.

"It's beautiful," she gasped.

"I hoped you'd think so. It was my mother's."

"Oh, Blade, I can't accept this."

"Please. I have a feeling she would have wanted you to have it." He clasped the chain around her neck as she continued to protest.

"It's much too valuable."

"So are you," he answered huskily. "What would I do without you?"

His smile had its usual effect, but Jessica had good reason to be skeptical. Blade had said that before, usually when they were in bed together. Was the necklace payment for services rendered?

She was immediately ashamed of herself. The fleeting thought was an insult to both of them. Blade would never be guilty of anything so crass. This was exactly how misunderstandings developed between them. He was actually giving her something that had great meaning to him.

"Thank you," she said simply. "I'll treasure it always."

He took her in his arms and stroked her hair gently, confirming Jessica's conviction that Blade's motives were pure. His embrace held deep affection rather than passion.

Their life together had always been a series of ups and downs, but after that misunderstanding they both tried hard to prevent another one from occurring.

They were only moderately successful. As the year slipped away, both were gripped by inner tension. Violent arguments would erupt between them over perfectly trivial matters. The battles would be followed by passionate reconciliations.

Their lovemaking became almost desperate as they tried to rouse each other to greater heights. Jessica would lie spent in Blade's arms, wondering how she was going to get through the rest of her life without him.

They never referred to the future, though. On the surface they pretended that time was unlimited and no change was imminent. Blade went to his job every day, and Jessica did hers. Kevin was happy, and all was apparently right with the world.

Nina didn't suspect their situation was less than perfect, although she and Jessica had become very friendly. Nina and Riley often came over on a weekend when they weren't catering a party, and the two couples spent a pleasant day together. Blade liked Riley and was won over by the change in Nina.

One day she phoned Jessica her voice quivering with excitement. "Guess what? Riley and I are getting married."

"That's wonderful news," Jessica exclaimed.

"I still can't believe it. I'm wearing a permanent smile."

"When is the happy event?"

"As soon as we can find a couple of free days for a honeymoon. Being successful has its drawbacks." Nina laughed.

"If you're that busy, maybe you should hire some people."

"We expect to, but we don't have time right now to train them."

"The way your company has taken off is fantastic. You must be really proud."

"*I* am," Nina answered tersely. "My mother is another story."

"What did she say when you told her?"

"I haven't yet. I thought I'd wait until after our second child is born. She could scarcely have the marriage annulled with little Dick and Jane clinging to my skirts."

"You're borrowing trouble. Sylvia will come around when she sees how happy you are."

"Do you also believe the tooth fairy is the one who pays out good money for all those disgusting little baby teeth?"

"Don't be so pessimistic. Your mother might surprise you."

"I'm not counting on it. But my wedding will take place with or without her," Nina said firmly.

"I want to hear all the details. Can you and Riley come over on the weekend? I know Blade will want to offer his congratulations, too."

"We're busy Saturday night and all day Sunday, but we could manage a couple of hours on Saturday afternoon if you're free."

"That will be fine. We'll look forward to seeing you," Jessica said.

Blade was as delighted as she at the news, but less optimistic about his aunt's eventual approval. "Nina better not tell her where the wedding is taking place. Sylvia might bomb the church."

"You and Nina are taking too negative a view. How could she help but like Riley?"

"It's simple. He works with his hands."

"So did Michelangelo."

"Too bad Riley doesn't do ceilings. The good news is that Sylvia is Nina's problem, not ours."

Sylvia became their problem a couple of nights later when she stormed in unexpectedly. Blade and Jessica were playing chess in the den.

"This is a surprise," he said tepidly. "Why didn't you let us know you were coming?"

"It isn't a social call." Her face was red with anger as she glared at Jessica. "I came to tell that woman what I think of her."

"What did I do?" Jessica asked blankly.

"Don't try to pretend innocence. Can you deny that you're responsible for Nina's bizarre behavior?"

"I honestly don't know what you're talking about," Jessica said.

"She would never have gotten involved in menial labor if you hadn't filled her head with ridiculous ideas. But even that wasn't enough for you. I know your kind fights dirty, but ruining a lovely girl's life to even a score with me is beneath contempt!"

"Now just a minute." Blade frowned.

"Let me handle this." Jessica faced the other woman calmly. "If you're referring to Nina's upcoming marriage, I had nothing to do with it. But I couldn't be more delighted, and you should be, too. Riley is a gem."

"You'd say that about any man," Sylvia sneered. She turned to Blade. "Don't you know about her by now?"

As his muscles tensed Jessica said quickly, "I thought we were talking about Nina's wedding."

"Which will never take place!" Sylvia flared. "I won't let her throw herself away on a ... an opportunist!"

"Your values are seriously skewed," Blade said tautly. "Your son is the one who's an opportunist, and your daughter wasn't much better before she met Riley O'Rourke. Luckily he glimpsed a real person under all the phoniness. Marrying him will be the most sensible thing Nina's done in her entire life."

"You're as responsible as Jessica for ruining my daughter's life," Sylvia said dramatically. "If you'd shared some of the money that should rightfully have been hers, she wouldn't be taking this drastic step."

"I hate to shoot down your righteous theory, but Nina won't accept anything she hasn't worked for. I offered them money to expand, and they both turned me down," Blade said.

"A pitiful sop to your conscience," she answered scornfully. "I'd be more impressed if you'd offered to pay that tradesman to stay away from her."

Blade shook his head disgustedly. "Leave them alone, Sylvia. They're in love."

"Is that what you call it? In my day we called it by its right name." Her eyes slanted toward Jessica. "And we certainly didn't throw away our prospects for it."

"I doubt if you'd ever let yourself be carried away by *any* human emotion," he answered contemptuously.

"And you are?" she asked, stung into renewed fury. "I don't notice *you* wasting yourself on a nobody! Advice is cheap when your own pleasure doesn't cost you anything."

Blade's face turned pale. "I seriously regret that you're not a man so I could beat the hell out of you," he grated. "Do yourself a favor and get out of here before I say something as stupid as you have."

After Sylvia left the air in the room still seemed to vibrate with the ugly words that had been hurled. Blade paced the floor with his fists jammed into his pockets.

"I'm sorry," he muttered. "You didn't deserve that. I wouldn't blame you if you walked out on the whole rotten bunch of us."

"Because of a couple of bad bananas?" Jessica tried to jolly him out of his black mood. Sylvia's unjustified attack had angered her, too, but Blade's defense was heartwarming.

"What can I do to make it up to you?" he asked somberly.

"You can stop letting Sylvia upset you."

"How can I when she's right about some things?"

"Are we talking about a woman who's so muddled she thinks her son is a responsible member of the human race?"

"How much better am I? I've taken advantage of your generosity without giving a thought to what it was costing you. I can't forgive myself for leaving you vulnerable to her filthy innuendos."

Jessica's face was serene. "Sylvia can't hurt me because I don't care what she thinks. I went into our relationship of my own free will, and I haven't been sorry. I'd hate to think you are."

"My darling Jessica." He framed her face in his palms and stared deeply into her eyes. "How could I be sorry for the happiest period of my life? Don't you know how I feel about you?"

"Tell me," she whispered. If ever the time was right it was now.

"You're as necessary to me as breathing. My life revolves around you. I'm happy all day long because I know you'll be here when I come home."

It was a declaration of love by any standards. Some men found it difficult to say the actual words, but the meaning was the same no matter how it was phrased.

"That's lovely, Blade." She clasped her arms around his neck.

He groaned as he reached up to loosen her grasp. "I don't want you to think this is all I care about, but I can't control myself when you do this."

"Silly man." She chuckled softly. "What makes you think I want you to?"

Growing excitement charged his body as he stared down at her. With one supple movement he lifted her into his arms and started for the stairs.

Afterward, lying contentedly in Blade's tender embrace, Jessica wondered if she had let a golden opportunity slip by. Would Blade finally have proposed? It was a distinct possibility after Sylvia's shabby accusations. But did she really want an offer triggered by guilt? It was better than no offer at all, a small voice answered.

Jessica stirred restlessly, not wanting anything to mar this golden moment. Right now, Blade belonged to her completely.

"Is something bothering you?" He was always attuned to her moods.

She tightened her arm around his waist and rubbed her cheek over the crisp hair on his chest. "Yes. The nights are too short."

His powerful frame relaxed at her answer, and his hand began to stroke her inner thigh in a sensual pattern. "Then we'll have to make the most of them," he murmured.

Jessica and Blade looked forward to the weekends when they could spend long hours alone together. Kevin had made so many friends that he usually had his own plans. That Saturday, though, he happened to be at loose ends.

"Let's go ice skating," he suggested. "We haven't done that in a long time."

"Not long enough for Jessica." Blade grinned at her.

"So I'm a klutz on ice." She shrugged. "Nobody can be good at everything."

"Your average is way up there," he said fondly.

Kevin waited them out with impatience. "If we can't go skating, let's go to the auto races. Johnny went last weekend, and he says they're neat. One car skidded off the track and turned over. Nobody got hurt, though."

"I'm sure Johnny was properly grateful," Blade remarked dryly.

"I don't know. Can we go?"

"Not today," Jessica answered. "Nina is coming over."

"You expect me to spend the day with *her*?" Kevin asked in outrage. In spite of Nina's overtures, he still hadn't accepted her.

"Relax. Your presence isn't required," Blade said.

"But I don't have anything to do today."

"Find something," Blade advised.

"We used to do things together," Kevin grumbled.

"Look, pal, don't try to lay a guilt trip on us just because you don't have any plans," Blade said. "You're usually off and running with your friends."

"They're all busy today," the boy complained.

"Then do something on your own. Take King for a run along the beach. You've been neglecting him lately. I told you he was your responsibility."

"Sheesh! You say one little thing and you get dumped on," Kevin remarked in an injured tone. "Come on, King, we know when we're not wanted around here."

"And brush him before you bring him back inside," Blade called as the dog bounded ahead of the youngster toward the door. "Mrs. Bartlett shouldn't have to vacuum up sand after him."

"Weren't you a little hard on him?" Jessica asked when they were alone.

"You spoil that kid rotten," Blade said affectionately.

"Who bought him the fancy camera equipment?" she countered.

"Okay, so we're both a couple of softies. But he has to learn that people aren't going to drop everything at his command. We wouldn't be doing him a favor if we let him believe that."

"You're right, of course," Jessica conceded. "I just worry that he'll feel rejected again."

"Children don't resent discipline as long as they know they're loved," Blade answered reassuringly.

Nina had never been beautiful, but she looked it that afternoon. There was a radiance about her when she looked at Riley, a softness that carried over to her personality.

"You've certainly done wonders for my little cousin," Blade told her fiancé. "She used to be somewhat of a pain in the posterior."

"Be careful how you talk about the woman I love," Riley responded. "I'd hate to have my best man show up at the wedding with a black eye."

Blade looked pleased. "Are you serious?"

Riley grinned and nodded. "About both offers."

"And I'd like you to be my maid of honor," Nina told Jessica.

Jessica hesitated. "I'd be delighted, but it might not be such a good idea. Sylvia would take a dim view of your choice."

"You're not the only one she disapproves of. Take a number and stand in line." Nina's happy face clouded over. "I don't think Mother will even be at my wedding. That was one of the ultimatums she gave me."

"Oh, Nina, I'm sure she'll reconsider."

"Who knows? Anyway, I still want you. Will you do it?"

"Of course, if you're sure," Jessica said. "Where are you planning to get married?"

Nina gave a short, humorless laugh. "I guess my parents' place is out. Maybe city hall."

"Would you like to be married here?" Jessica asked gently.

Nina brightened. "Could we? Would you mind, Blade?"

He smiled. "I won't even ask you to cater it."

"You're going to hire the competition?" Riley joked. "Unless you want to get married in his and her matching aprons."

"Will you wear a formal wedding gown?" Jessica asked Nina.

"Nothing that elaborate. We want an afternoon ceremony. I was thinking about a suit or a dress with a jacket."

"I saw a beautiful short white chiffon dress with a lace top in one of the fashion magazines," Jessica said. "It would look stunning on you."

"You think that's a better choice than a cocktail suit?"

"They're starting to talk a foreign language," Blade said to Riley. "Let's drive to the Wharf and pick up some fresh crab."

"Sure. Nothing I like better than shopping for food on my day off," Riley grumbled good-naturedly as he followed Blade out of the room.

Jessica brought out her fashion magazines, and the two women leafed through them. They were too engrossed to notice when Kevin peered through the open window, and he ducked down before they had a second chance. He sat on the steps and started to brush the shaggy coat of the now tremendous dog.

When they'd pretty well exhausted the subject of clothes Jessica and Nina switched to wedding arrangements.

"This is such fun," Jessica remarked. "I never planned a wedding before."

"Who would ever have thought it would be mine instead of yours?"

"*I* would," Jessica answered tersely.

"Blade's a chump," Nina said disgustedly.

"And you're a romantic. I told you my arrangement here was just a temporary one."

"What will you do when you leave?" Nina asked.

"I don't know. Travel for a while perhaps, then get another job."

"How about Blade? You think he'll go back overseas to live at the end of the year?"

"I know he will," Jessica answered quietly.

On the steps under the window the small boy suddenly became motionless.

"How about Kevin?" Nina persisted.

"He'll stay on here, I assume. The will only set conditions for one year."

"I still can't get over Uncle Winston's will," Nina mused. "I'm not surprised that he cut my family and me out, but what he did to you two was weird."

"Most people would think he was very generous to me," Jessica said ironically. "Mr. Dunsmuir paid me a lot of money to come and live here."

"I'll bet Blade wasn't as grateful. He had to give up a job he loved, and take on a lot of responsibilities besides."

"Blade was paid well, too," Jessica said evenly. "We both had to make adjustments, but nothing is forever. The year is almost up."

Kevin's face was very pale under his tan as he stood up and walked quietly down the stairs to the beach.

"I can't believe you won't be here," Nina said forlornly. "I know it's crazy since we had such a rocky beginning, but I consider you my best friend."

"We'll keep in touch," Jessica promised, wondering if she really would.

"It won't be the same, though, without Blade."

"No, it will never be like this again," Jessica agreed soberly.

She made a determined effort to put melancholy behind her when the men returned. Blade opened a bottle of champagne, and they toasted the happy couple.

"We really shouldn't be doing this," Nina said, holding out her glass for a refill, nonetheless. "What if we serve the courses out of order or use the wrong seasoning?"

"Tell them it's a new kind of cuisine," Blade advised. "Californians will eat anything if they think it's avant-garde."

After Nina and Riley had left, Jessica and Blade discussed the coming event.

"Do you think Sylvia will relent?" Jessica asked.

He shrugged. "As far as I'm concerned, she can stay home and read the social register."

"Nina would be so hurt, even though she pretends not to care. I know I'd be crushed under the same circumstances."

"If Sylvia does come, I'm going to hold Carter personally responsible for keeping her in line. He's one person I can take on," Blade said ominously.

Jessica smiled. "No, you can't. He's an older man, and he's your uncle."

"Only by marriage. That ought to entitle me to get in a few licks."

"You're all bark and no bite," she teased. "It was sweet of you to let Nina be married here."

"What could I do about it? You'd already offered."

"You don't really mind, do you?" she asked uncertainly.

"You know I don't, angel. It will be one more happy memory." His smile faded as they gazed at each other.

That was happening more and more often. Jessica changed the subject hurriedly. "I wonder where Kevin is? I haven't seen him all afternoon."

"He'll show up for dinner. How about taking him to a movie tonight?"

"Good idea. I'll get the newspaper and we'll pick out something suitable."

Blade grinned. "Your idea of suitable and his idea are apt to differ."

"No slasher movies," she said firmly. "You have to back me up on that one."

"How about something sexy like *Teens in Tight Jeans*?" he teased.

"I can see I'll have to choose this movie alone."

Blade looked at his watch a little later and frowned. "Where is that boy? It's almost dinnertime."

Jessica felt a stirring of uneasiness. "It isn't like him to stay away so long without telling us where he was going."

"He probably told Mrs. B."

They both went to the kitchen to speak to the house-keeper, but she didn't know any more than they did.

"Have you looked in his room?" she asked. "When that child starts playing his tapes he's in another world."

"Of course." Jessica's tension drained away. "Why didn't we think of that?"

But no music assaulted them in the upstairs hall, and Kevin's room was empty. The very neatness seemed om-inous, although Jessica reminded herself that Mrs. Bart-lett had straightened up after him.

"Where could he be?" she faltered.

"Probably at Johnny's house." If Blade shared her uneasiness, he didn't allow it to show. "That young man is due for a lecture on responsibility."

Kevin wasn't at Johnny's or with any of his other friends. When Blade put down the phone after calling the last person they could think of, his face was lined.

"You'd better call the police," Jessica whispered.

"They won't do anything this soon. He's only been gone a few hours."

"We haven't seen him since lunchtime. That's all afternoon."

"All right, if it will make you feel better," he said casually.

But Blade was correct. The police sergeant informed him that a person wasn't considered missing until he'd been gone for twenty-four hours.

"My own kid never knows when it's time to come home," the man told Blade indulgently. "He'll turn up, Mr. Dunsmuir."

"Oh, Blade, what are we going to do?" Jessica stared at him wide-eyed.

"We're going to look for him," he said firmly. "Maybe he's down on the beach working on that fort of his. He could simply have lost track of time."

Jessica knew Blade was as worried as she, but he was keeping up appearances for her sake. The least she could do was not add to his burden.

She forced her voice to remain calm. "You could be right. He's obsessed with that fort."

As they started down the back steps, a wire brush clattered to the ground. "King must be with him," Blade said. "If he has that big brute along, nothing can happen to him."

Jessica had a momentary feeling of relief, but it didn't last long. The fort was empty and fog was rolling in, blurring the distant houses on the bluff. The fog would grow thicker, obscuring even the ocean that was encroaching on the beach as it reached high tide. If a little boy and a dog had gotten caught in the powerful undertow of those angry waves, maybe to retrieve a stick . . . Jessica felt panic rising in her throat.

"Kevin!" she shouted suddenly, running toward the water. "Kevin, where are you?" Her plea was flung back in her face by the wind.

Blade's hands grasped her shoulders. "We'll find him. Maybe he fell climbing on he rocks, but he's all right. He's out there waiting for us, and we'll find him."

As Blade's strength seeped into her she forced down her fear and nodded. "We'd better split up. We can cover more territory that way."

"You're right." He squeezed her hand briefly and strode away.

Jessica took the other direction. Turning away from the beach, she climbed up a sloping path covered with ice plant. The stems were tangled and woody. They could trap an unwary foot and twist an ankle. She scanned the broad expanse intently, her heart pounding at every imagined discovery. But each proved to be a scrap of cloth, a discarded fast-food container or some other debris.

At the top of the hill were large houses and tree-lined streets. Jessica thought of knocking on doors to ask if anyone had seen a little boy in the neighborhood that afternoon. But the chance was slim, and she didn't want to waste time on explanations. The vision of Kevin lying hurt and helpless somewhere made her teeth clench painfully. She did question a man walking his dog. He would be apt to remember King, at least.

"No, I haven't seen them," he said. "Have you looked along the cliff? Youngsters love to play around up there. I shoo them away all the time because it's dangerous for them."

Jessica thanked him and continued her search, far from reassured. The gentle slope she'd climbed became steeper higher up. The backyards of the houses built along the rising hill dropped away to a narrow path that wound along the top of the cliff facing the ocean. At the bottom of a sheer drop were jagged rocks washed by waves pounding against the granite wall.

Jessica shivered as she started up the slippery path. The temperature had dropped and the fog was thicker now. Her breath caught in her throat when she stumbled and sprawled perilously close to the edge, but she got up and plodded on, calling Kevin's name at intervals.

Time lost all meaning. Only her cold, numbed body told her she'd been out there a long time. Suddenly a gazebo swam out of the fog like a mirage. It was patterned after a Greek temple with graceful pillars and a domed roof. Jessica longed to get out of the wind for a few minutes, but she couldn't permit herself the luxury.

Then like a miracle, a large white shape came bounding toward her, and a deep bark told Jessica her search was ended. At least half of it was. She raced up to the summerhouse, her nerves stretched to the breaking point. Inside was a small figure huddled on the ground.

"Kevin! Thank God!" Jessica went down on her knees and took him in her arms. "Are you all right?"

He twisted away from her. "Let go of me."

"What are you doing here? Do you know how worried we've been?"

"Sure, I'll bet," he sneered.

She looked at him in bewilderment. "What's wrong, Kevin? Why did you scare us this way? Was it because we didn't take you skating today?"

"I don't care about that. I don't ever want to do anything with you again!"

"You have to tell me why."

"What difference does it make? You never cared about me, either of you."

"That's not true! Your uncle and I love you very much."

"Is that why you're both going away and leaving me?"

She drew in her breath sharply. "Where did you hear that?"

"From you. I heard you talking to Nina today. I know all about how you were paid to take care of me. Neither one of you wanted to. You just pretended to like me because of the money."

"You're so wrong," she said urgently. "That had absolutely nothing to do with you."

"You're just saying that, but I'm not stupid. I was outside the window."

"You have to believe me, Kevin. You completely misunderstood those things you heard."

"You're not going away?" Hope seeped into his voice.

As she groped for the right words to make him understand Jessica became aware that his teeth were chattering. "I've never lied to you, Kevin, and I won't now. But we have to go home and get you into some warm clothes before you catch pneumonia. After that I'll explain everything, I promise."

Mrs. Bartlett was limp with relief when they reached home. She was filled with questions, but Jessica reserved her answers until after Kevin had gone upstairs with instructions to take a hot shower and get into bed.

"I'll fix the poor little lad some dinner," the housekeeper said. "He must be starved."

"It's Blade I'm worried about," Jessica said. "He's probably frantic by now."

"Hawkins went out to look for him," Mrs. Bartlett soothed. "Everything's going to be all right."

Jessica climbed the stairs somberly, searching for the right words to say to Kevin.

He was getting into bed as she entered his room. The pinched look was gone from his face, but his eyes lacked their usual sparkle. Jessica sat down on the bed and tucked the covers around him.

"I'm sorry you didn't come to me when you were upset. You could have spared everyone a lot of anxiety, most of all yourself. It's true that your uncle and I are leaving shortly, but that doesn't mean we don't love you."

"If you did, you'd stay." His chin quivered.

"People can't always do what they want. Blade has a job to go back to, a very important job. He left it to come home and take care of you."

"Yeah, because he was paid to. I heard you say so."

Jessica bitterly regretted her ironic remark. "Your grandfather's will said he had to live here for a year," she admitted. "But he could have spent this year a lot differently. He didn't have to worry about your happiness. Why do you think he bought you a dog and taught you to skate and took you to the movies? He devoted all his time to you when you needed him. Does that sound like he doesn't love you?"

Kevin had grown increasingly penitent as she recited Blade's many thoughtful acts. "Will I ever see him again after he leaves?" he asked wistfully.

"Oh, darling, of course you will! Blade told me himself that he expects to come home for holidays whenever he can. And maybe you can go to visit him during summer vacation. You could get on an airplane all by yourself. Wouldn't that be exciting?"

"Do you think he'd really let me?" Kevin was no longer as subdued.

"I wouldn't doubt it a bit. He's going to miss you terribly."

"Can I ask him now?"

"As soon as he comes home," Jessica promised.

She didn't know that Blade had already returned. Relief hadn't yet erased the worry lines from his face. He had to see Kevin to reassure himself.

"You're cold and wet, Mr. Blade," the housekeeper fretted. "Let me fix you a hot toddy to warm you up."

"Later, Mrs. Bartlett."

He took the stairs two at a time, but as he hurried down the long hall toward Kevin's room, the conversation inside stopped him in his tracks.

"Maybe I understand why Uncle Blade has to leave, but couldn't you stay with me?"

"No. My job here is over," Jessica said quietly.

"I could pay you," the little boy said eagerly. "Cousin Larry said I have more money than I can spend. But if I don't have enough, Uncle Blade would pay you. I know he would."

"I don't want your money, Kevin, and I don't want his," she said sadly. "Blade always thought I did, that was the trouble. If only he'd been poor." She sighed.

"Don't you like Uncle Blade the way he is?" he asked uncertainly.

"I love him," she answered simply. "That's why I'm going away. You're too young to understand now, but you will someday."

The finality in her voice told Kevin it was useless to argue. "Will you come to see me?" he asked plaintively.

"Not right away." She didn't want to lie to him. "It would be too painful to relive the memories. That's another thing you'll understand when you're older. But if you ever need me, I'll come in a minute. Always remember that.''

"I don't want you to go, Jessica.'' Tears rolled down his cheeks.

"She isn't going anywhere.'' Blade strode into the room, his entire body charged with energy.

"Blade!'' The color drained from her cheeks. "How long have you been out there?''

"Long enough to realize what a fool I've been.''

She stood up slowly. "I never wanted you to know. But in a way, I'm glad. At least you know now that you were wrong about me. The money was important to you, never to me.''

"It's amazing how two people who love each other can get so far off the track.'' As she stared at him, afraid to believe what she'd heard, Blade walked toward her. "We have a lot of misconceptions to clear up.''

"Do you really mean it, Uncle Blade?'' Kevin tugged at his sleeve. "Is Jessica really staying with me?''

Blade gave him a dazzling smile. "Except for a brief honeymoon. But you wouldn't begrudge us that, would you, pal?''

Jessica was gazing speechlessly at him when Mrs. Bartlett came in carrying a supper tray for Kevin.

"The soup is nice and hot,'' she announced. "Can I fix a bowl for the two of you?''

It was Kevin who answered excitedly, "They're getting married, and Jessica is going to keep on living here, and Uncle Blade will come home on holidays.''

"Is that a fact?'' The older woman didn't look surprised.

Blade laughed. "I expect to do better than that. Jessica and I are about to work out the details.''

She followed him down the hall wordlessly, trying to make sense out of what was happening.

When the door of his bedroom closed behind them he took her in his arms. "You will marry me, won't you, angel?"

She stared at him searchingly. "You mean right away?"

The elation drained out of his face. "It's that damn will again, isn't it? Are we going to go on letting it ruin our lives? I love you, Jessica. Don't you know that by now?"

Every instinct urged her to say yes, but she had to bring her suspicions out in the open. They'd kept things hidden from each other for too long. "You've made a lot of sacrifices for the money," she said slowly.

"The inference being that I wouldn't stop at one more? You're so wrong, my love. Would you be convinced if I told you I never wanted the money for myself?"

"What do you mean?"

"I told you about the suffering I saw overseas. I never got hardened to it, especially what war does to small children. With generous checks from my father and contributions from other people with a conscience, I set up an orphanage for those poor little kids. The money I'll inherit is vitally needed. That's why I agreed to the conditions of Dad's will. It's also the reason I have to go back there, for a short time at least, to see that everything is running properly."

"Why didn't you tell me?" Jessica exclaimed, even as the reason was clear. They'd created their own problems; the will wasn't responsible. "We've wasted so much time," she said regretfully.

"Not compared to the rest of our lives. Will you marry me, Jessica"

She flung her arms around his neck. "How about to-morrow morning?"

He drew back to look at her gravely. "I didn't mean before the year was up."

"If you think I'm going to wait that long you're badly mistaken."

"It's only a few weeks," he said tentatively. "That's a small price to pay for resolving any doubts you might have."

"If it weren't for the will, would you marry me to-morrow?"

"It's what I want more than anything in the world," he said fervently, crushing her almost fiercely in his arms.

"You're luckier than most people." She smiled enchantingly. "You're going to get your wish."

Epilogue

The letter was delivered to their hotel suite while Jessica and Blade were having a late breakfast. Blade slit open the envelope without much interest.

"Who is it from?" Jessica asked.

"Grant Sutherland. Wouldn't you think business could wait till we got back from our honeymoon?" he grumbled. But his face sobered when he began to read what was inside.

"Is anything wrong?" she asked.

"He sent me a letter from my father," Blade answered slowly. "To be opened in the event of our marriage. Listen to this:

'My dear children, if you've received this letter, it means my fondest wish has been realized. I always knew you were perfect for each other, and now you've found that out for yourselves.

You were probably furious over the conditions of my will, but that was the best way I knew of to bring you together. The mutual attraction between you was so obvious, yet you were both too stubborn to admit it. You needed time to get to know and love each other the way I love both of you.

Have a happy life, my dear children, and if you can't think of a better name for your first son, I'd be very proud if you named him after me.'

"Can you believe the way he manipulated us?" Blade exclaimed as he flung the letter down. "My father almost ruined our lives! It's no thanks to him that everything turned out all right."

"He knew us better than we knew ourselves, and he had faith in us," Jessica said softly. "We owe him a great deal."

Blade's indignation died as he cradled her chin in his palm and gazed at her with deep love. "There's only one thing we can give him. Would you care to discuss it?"

"Gladly." She put her arms around his neck and raised her face for his kiss. "But what he asked for doesn't require a lot of conversation."

* * * * *

Silhouette Special Edition

COMING NEXT MONTH

#589 INTIMATE CIRCLE—Curtiss Ann Matlock
Their passion was forbidden, suspect . . . silenced by the specter of his late
brother—her husband. Could Rachel and Dallas reweave the angry,
fragmented Cordell and Tyson clans into a warming circle of love?

#590 CLOSE RANGE—Elizabeth Bevarly
Tough, disillusioned P.I. Mick Dante had long admired ethereal neighbor
Emily Thorne from afar. But when she approached him to track her
missing brother, temptation—and trouble!—zoomed into *very* close range.

#591 PLACES IN THE HEART—Andrea Edwards
When Matt finally came home, he discovered he'd relinquished far more
than he'd imagined. . . . But would Tessa make room in her heart for her
late husband, her sons, *and* the lover who'd once left her behind?

#592 FOREVER YOUNG—Elaine Lakso
Levelheaded Tess DeSain ran the family bakery—and her life—quietly,
sensibly . . . until flamboyant Ben Young barged into both, brazenly
enticing her to have her cake and eat it, too!

#593 KINDRED SPIRITS—Sarah Temple
Running from Ian Craddock's dangerously attractive intensity, Tara
Alladyce sought emotional sanctuary . . . in a phantom fling. But Ian
wasn't giving up easily—he'd brave man, beast *or* spirit to win her back!

#594 SUDDENLY, PARADISE—Jennifer West
Nomadic Annie Adderly kept her tragic past a secret . . . and kept running.
Then incisive, sensual detective Chris Farrentino began penetrating her
cover, pressing for clues, probing altogether too deeply. . . .

AVAILABLE THIS MONTH:

#583 TAMING NATASHA
Nora Roberts

#584 WILLING PARTNERS
Tracy Sinclair

#585 PRIVATE WAGERS
Betsy Johnson

#586 A GUILTY PASSION
Laurey Bright

#587 HOOPS
Patricia McLinn

#588 SUMMER'S FREEDOM
Ruth Wind

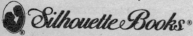

You'll flip . . . your pages won't!
Read paperbacks *hands-free* with

Book Mate • I

The perfect "mate" for all your romance paperbacks

Traveling • Vacationing • At Work • In Bed • Studying • Cooking • Eating

Perfect size for all standard paperbacks, this wonderful invention makes reading a pure pleasure! Ingenious design holds paperback books OPEN and FLAT so even wind can't ruffle pages — leaves your hands free to do other things. Reinforced, wipe-clean vinyl-covered holder flexes to let you turn pages without undoing the strap . . . supports paperbacks so well, they have the strength of hardcovers!

Pages turn WITHOUT opening the strap

SEE-THROUGH STRAP

Reinforced back stays flat

Built in bookmark

BOOK MARK

BACK COVER HOLDING STRIP

10 x 7¼ opened.
Snaps closed for easy carrying, too

Available now. Send your name, address, and zip code, along with a check or money order for just $5.95 + .75¢ for postage & handling (for a total of $6.70) payable to Reader Service to:

Reader Service
Bookmate Offer
901 Fuhrmann Blvd.
P.O. Box 1396
Buffalo, N.Y. 14269-1396

Offer not available in Canada
*New York and Iowa residents add appropriate sales tax.

BM-G

Silhouette Special Edition®

proudly presents

Taming Natasha
by
NORA ROBERTS

Once again, award-winning author Nora Roberts weaves her special brand of magic this month in TAMING NATASHA (SSE #583). Toy shop owner Natasha Stanislaski is a pussycat with Spence Kimball's little girl, but to Spence himself she's as ornery as a caged tiger. Will some cautious loving sheath her claws and free her heart from captivity?

TAMING NATASHA, by Nora Roberts, has been selected to receive a special laurel—the Award of Excellence. This month look for the distinctive emblem on the cover. It lets you know there's something truly special inside.

Available now

TAME-1A

A celebration of motherhood by three of your favorite authors!

Birds, Bees and Babies

JENNIFER GREENE
KAREN KEAST
EMILIE RICHARDS

This May, expect something wonderful from Silhouette Books — BIRDS, BEES AND BABIES — a collection of three heartwarming stories bundled into one very special book.

It's a lullaby of love . . . dedicated to the romance of motherhood.

Look for BIRDS, BEES AND BABIES in May at your favorite retail outlet.

®

BBB-1